A

MURDER

IN

PARIS

(A Year in Europe—Book 1)

BLAKE PIERCE

Blake Pierce

Blake Pierce is the USA Today bestselling author of the RILEY PAGE mystery series, which includes seventeen books. Blake Pierce is also the author of the MACKENZIE WHITE mystery series, comprising fourteen books; of the AVERY BLACK mystery series, comprising six books; of the KERI LOCKE mystery series, comprising five books; of the MAKING OF RILEY PAIGE mystery series, comprising six books; of the KATE WISE mystery series, comprising seven books; of the CHLOE FINE psychological suspense mystery, comprising six books; of the JESSE HUNT psychological suspense thriller series, comprising fifteen books (and counting); of the AU PAIR psychological suspense thriller series, comprising three books; of the ZOE PRIME mystery series, comprising six books; of the ADELE SHARP mystery series, comprising ten books (and counting); of the EUROPEAN VOYAGE cozy mystery series, comprising six books (and counting); of the new LAURA FROST FBI suspense thriller, comprising three books (and counting); of the new ELLA DARK FBI suspense thriller, comprising six books (and counting); of the A YEAR IN EUROPE cozy mystery series, comprising three books (and counting); of the AVA GOLD mystery series, comprising three books (and counting); and of the RACHEL GIFT mystery series, comprising three books (and counting).

An avid reader and lifelong fan of the mystery and thriller genres, Blake loves to hear from you, so please feel free to visit www.blakepierceauthor.com to learn more and stay in touch.

THE PERFECT DECEIT (Book #14)
THE PERFECT MISTRESS (Book #15)

CHLOE FINE PSYCHOLOGICAL SUSPENSE SERIES
NEXT DOOR (Book #1)
A NEIGHBOR'S LIE (Book #2)
CUL DE SAC (Book #3)
SILENT NEIGHBOR (Book #4)
HOMECOMING (Book #5)
TINTED WINDOWS (Book #6)

KATE WISE MYSTERY SERIES
IF SHE KNEW (Book #1)
IF SHE SAW (Book #2)
IF SHE RAN (Book #3)
IF SHE HID (Book #4)
IF SHE FLED (Book #5)
IF SHE FEARED (Book #6)
IF SHE HEARD (Book #7)

THE MAKING OF RILEY PAIGE SERIES
WATCHING (Book #1)
WAITING (Book #2)
LURING (Book #3)
TAKING (Book #4)
STALKING (Book #5)
KILLING (Book #6)

RILEY PAIGE MYSTERY SERIES
ONCE GONE (Book #1)
ONCE TAKEN (Book #2)
ONCE CRAVED (Book #3)
ONCE LURED (Book #4)
ONCE HUNTED (Book #5)
ONCE PINED (Book #6)
ONCE FORSAKEN (Book #7)
ONCE COLD (Book #8)
ONCE STALKED (Book #9)
ONCE LOST (Book #10)

ONCE BURIED (Book #11)
ONCE BOUND (Book #12)
ONCE TRAPPED (Book #13)
ONCE DORMANT (Book #14)
ONCE SHUNNED (Book #15)
ONCE MISSED (Book #16)
ONCE CHOSEN (Book #17)

MACKENZIE WHITE MYSTERY SERIES
BEFORE HE KILLS (Book #1)
BEFORE HE SEES (Book #2)
BEFORE HE COVETS (Book #3)
BEFORE HE TAKES (Book #4)
BEFORE HE NEEDS (Book #5)
BEFORE HE FEELS (Book #6)
BEFORE HE SINS (Book #7)
BEFORE HE HUNTS (Book #8)
BEFORE HE PREYS (Book #9)
BEFORE HE LONGS (Book #10)
BEFORE HE LAPSES (Book #11)
BEFORE HE ENVIES (Book #12)
BEFORE HE STALKS (Book #13)
BEFORE HE HARMS (Book #14)

AVERY BLACK MYSTERY SERIES
CAUSE TO KILL (Book #1)
CAUSE TO RUN (Book #2)
CAUSE TO HIDE (Book #3)
CAUSE TO FEAR (Book #4)
CAUSE TO SAVE (Book #5)
CAUSE TO DREAD (Book #6)

KERI LOCKE MYSTERY SERIES
A TRACE OF DEATH (Book #1)
A TRACE OF MUDER (Book #2)
A TRACE OF VICE (Book #3)
A TRACE OF CRIME (Book #4)
A TRACE OF HOPE (Book #5)

CHAPTER ONE

Sipping from her *I Survived Another Meeting That Should Have Been an Email* coffee mug, Diana St. James shivered in the too-chilly air-conditioning. Who'd turned that sucker down again?

Someone on the floor definitely had the constitution of a penguin just like her soon-to-be ex-husband, Evan. All those years, she'd had to grin and bear it when he turned the thermostat *way* down. It was *so* much better to be able to do as one pleased, organize the house the way she wanted to . . . *I should be happy to be getting rid of him!*

Diana stood behind her desk, contemplating the latest addition to the product line. Sure, there was MAC cosmetics, NARS cosmetics, e.l.f., and NYX. But the last thing they needed was to make Addict the *butt* of all jokes by naming their latest, greatest mascara after one.

B. U. T. Who the heck came up with that one?

Diana sighed. It was another rainy Monday. It seemed like April showers had just given way to *more* May showers, and now it was a humid, sticky, waterlogged early June. The floor-to-ceiling windows in Diana's corner office were steamed over, only partially blocking her view of the throngs of people dodging the puddles and raindrops on the busy Tribeca street below.

She went to her intercom and buzzed Sandy, her trusty, just-out-of-college administrative assistant. Diana had chosen her because, with her blue eyes and freckles, she reminded her of her youngest daughter, Beatrice, who'd been in Japan for the past year. Most marketing executives would've questioned that hiring move—god knows, HR did, especially since Sandy didn't have squat on her resume—but Diana hadn't had the heart or the time to go through a lengthy hiring process. Anyway, it had turned out to be a good decision. Sandy was always cheerful, always willing to help, and always eager to learn.

Plus, she always answered on the first buzz. "Good morning, Diana! How can I help?"

1

"Hi, Sandy. Can you please tell Phil that none of these names is going to work for the new mascara? They're going to have to go back to the drawing board and come up with something different."

"Oh, really? Because I thought that B.U.T. one was cute! Ellie in graphic design came up with that," she said in her too-happy-for-Monday voice. "Get it? Like, *B-U-T*. Beauty?"

"I understand that," Diana said with a wan smile, "But the last thing we want is anyone to associate Addict's latest product with one's derriere. Right?"

"Oh. Yes. I understand. Good point. I'll tell him. Right away."

"Thank you. See if they can come up with anything new before the morning meeting," she said, depressing the button and sighing as she scooted forward in her leather executive chair. Opening her email, she started to go through the two hundred that Sandy had flagged for her as *Urgent*.

This was nothing new. She'd been the marketing director for Addict for over twenty years, almost since its inception, so now she ate, slept, and breathed the products. In the beginning when she was new to the company—though she'd been a marketing manager at Elizabeth Arden for ten years prior—Addict was young, hip, and fun; but now it was exclusive, refined, and sold at high-end boutiques. It had aged right along with the women it served. A few years ago, against Diana's better judgement, they'd tried to take back some market share among teenagers, even hiring a young YouTube star as their spokesperson—and what a disaster that had been.

Now, Diana knew to trust her instincts. And her instincts were clearly saying N.O. to B.U.T. or any of their other less-than-buzzworthy ideas.

After tackling the first few emails, a meeting alert popped up on the corner of her computer screen, telling her it was time for the morning briefing. Leaving her mug on her desk, she grabbed her pen and blank pad and headed next door to the massive board room. On the way, she mentally ran through ideas for the mascara line. *Lash Pump? Lethal Lengths? Incredi-Pop? Really, anything would be better than B.U.T.*

Her staff was already assembled, chatting. They quieted down when she came in. She wasn't sure if that was something they did around all the executives, out of respect, or just around her, out of fear. She tried to be relatable and fun—and thought they liked her, but a supervisor never could tell what her employees whispered about around the water cooler. It didn't matter. She wasn't there to be their friends. If they didn't like her, they all did a good job of faking it, smiling and saying "good morning" as she sat at the head of the table.

As she pulled her chair in, she let out a sigh. Same scenery, different week.

"Hello, everyone. And how was your weekend?" she said, just as a formality. She didn't care to know, and she sensed from their usual terse responses that they understood that.

They all nodded and added their own version of "too short." Short? Really, they didn't know the meaning of the word. At least they'd left the office for more than a few hours. Diana hadn't. She'd stayed overnight Sunday into Monday, working on the new spreads for their *Allure* ad, and showered in the downstairs gym. She kept an entire closet of clothes in her office just for that purpose. So while her employees may have had lives outside of the Addict headquarters, Diana—well—didn't. Not anymore, anyway.

Among the group of twelve, a third were millennials. She related to them because of her own daughters. The rest were older, in their thirties and forties. And then there was Phil, branding director, who had come on board around the same time Diana had and was nearly Diana's age. The two had clawed at each other, years ago, over who'd become a senior vice president and lead the creative group. She'd managed to come out on top.

Still full of piss and vinegar over the snub, Phil wasn't going to be happy about her nixing all those brand-name ideas. But she'd been through that rodeo before. She knew how to cut through his crap.

"How was yours?" he asked from his usual spot at her right elbow. He was busy nursing his usual extra-huge commuter cup of something, probably a necessity due to his commute in from Central Jersey. "Do anything fun?" he questioned in a lilting way that made her wince. He knew she hadn't.

"Yes. It was fun. Quiet," she said, not looking at him. Though she'd tried to keep the messy details of her pending divorce out of the office, it had a way of leaking in, anyhow. With all the phone calls Sandy had been taking from her lawyer and Evan, they likely knew *something* was up. She pointed to her notebook. After decades of running these meetings, she knew the agenda by heart, but she never came in without one. She couldn't afford to let anything sidetrack her from the work that needed to be done, and side-conversations and tangents always seemed to bloat meetings unnecessarily. "Let's get start—"

She stopped when she realized she didn't have the full attention of the room. A few of the millennials on the other side, Sandy included, were speaking in a low voice to one another, grinning. The three stopped talking and looked at Diana. "Sorry," Sandy mumbled.

"Am I missing something?" Diana asked. Sometimes this was like dealing with a bunch of kids. *Anything you'd like to share with the class?*

Sandy shook her head, "Marie was just telling us about her amazing vacation."

Case in point—the vacation tangent, that was the last thing this meeting needed. People always seemed to go on about them—where they were going, where they'd been, et cetera, et cetera. As if being at work was so awful, they'd rather talk of anyplace else.

"Perhaps you can discuss that after the meeting," she said with a smile.

Sandy nodded, "Yes. Of course. I just wanted to know where she got that banging bracelet."

Macey, the willowy, messy-bun-wearing blonde from graphic design, always wore black turtlenecks, even in the dead of summer. Now, she was wearing a bright red cuff with gold accents that was quite attractive. Not only that, but she had that just-back-from-vacation glow in her high cheekbones. Diana rarely paid much attention to the graphic designers since they were always squirreled away behind their massive Mac screens, but Macey had once looked sickly—exhausted. Now it was like she was a different person. She had to admit it was infectious.

Being young and in love and away from the daily grind can do that for you. I was there, once.

That was why they gave them four weeks of PTO to start. Diana had unlimited days off, but she couldn't remember the last time she'd used a single day. She was planning to skip this year's vacation, much like last year, and the year before. Something about sitting alone on a beach, while honeymooning couples traipsed around her, felt like torture. "Oh? You went to the islands with Blake, did you?"

"Actually, my boyfriend had to work. I decided to take a solo trip. I hiked the mountains in Spain. You know, to clear my head," Macey responded, holding up her wrist, the cuff jingling along with the other jewelry she had on. "And a craftsman was selling these in a little hut on the side of the road. Sixty euros."

"Oh?" Diana asked, flabbergasted. One could *do* that—just head out on one's own? Macey had never sounded like the brave soul who'd solo vacation anywhere. In fact, she and the other girls usually didn't venture to the *bathroom* unless they were in a group. A whole other country? She had to give her props. "And did you clear your head?"

"Oh, my gosh, yes!" the young woman gushed, smiling broadly and patting her heart as if it were about to explode from her chest. "It was amazing. I learned so much about the country. About myself. I'd do it again in a heartbeat."

A little thrill stuttered through Diana's own heart. Forgetting the boardroom walls surrounding her and the rest of her group lined up around the table, she blurted, "Really? And you did it entirely on your own? You didn't know anyone?"

"Not a single person on the entire *continent*. And I flunked Spanish in school. So it was really intimidating at first," she laughed. "Half the time, I didn't know what anyone was saying!"

"And you weren't scared?"

"To be honest, I was *terrified*."

Diana nodded, understanding. Even at just over fifty, she would've been scared, too. When was the last time she'd traveled alone, anywhere? Oh, Evan liked his vacations, but he usually chose those all-inclusive beach resort things, where their only responsibility was showing up and the staff took it from there. As a surgeon, he was used to using his brain so much at work that he didn't want to have to use it on his vacations. Then, with the kids in tow, they'd gone to Disney, the Jersey Shore, or OBX. She'd never even entertained the thought of going out by herself. Some days, it was hard enough getting five minutes to herself. An entire "alone" trip? Insane.

Well, it hadn't been *that* insane of an idea—when she was younger like Macey. She would've entertained such an idea with no qualms, once. Decades ago. Before Evan came and swept her off her feet, she'd had all those plans. Her biggest one? Paris. More specifically, Versailles.

Oh, yes. She'd taken seven years of French in high school and college—committing to memory things like *comment allez-vous* and *où sont les toilettes?*—just waiting for the day when she'd be out on her own, able to travel the world. Right before she'd graduated from NYU,

5

it all seemed to be coming true. The world, her oyster. She'd gotten that coveted invitation to the masquerade ball, from a dashing Frenchman. And then . . .

Major wrench—career, Evan, kids—all those early plans gone. Long years had passed. Now there was barely anything left of that idealistic girl.

"But you have to understand . . . I was only nervous at first," Macey continued. "By the time I stepped off the plane, I was fine. People love to help tourists. Everyone was so nice. You make a lot of friends with other solo travelers. I got lost a few times, sure. But I had a total blast and made it back in one piece."

That was what her youngest daughter, Beatrice, had said when, a year ago, she up and went to Japan after graduating with her master's degree. *Don't worry. Everyone here is so nice!* She'd assured Diana of that without the least bit of trepidation at all. Diana had felt enough for the two of them . . . or maybe that was a tiny splash of envy?

Which reminded her. She had to call Bea.

Diana stared at Macey until she realized her mouth was hanging open. The entire room seemed to have darkened under shadow, becoming more depressing, the walls closing in. As she scanned the faces of the people around the massive boardroom table, she suddenly remembered her purpose.

"Oh. Nice," she said, trying not to leak any of the jealousy that was currently bubbling inside her. "Glad to have you back, Macey. Now, let's start with number one on the agenda. The name for the new mascara."

She glared at Phil, who smirked, "I thought the ones we came up with showed promise."

"Phil. Honestly? They're terrible."

"You have any better ideas?"

She opened her mouth, ready to tell him the handful of ideas she'd come up with during her ten-second brainstorming session earlier.

But suddenly, an image popped into her head of her at outdoor café enjoying a French pastry while romantic music swelled and the Eiffel Tower rose up in the background.

And she realized she couldn't remember a single one of her names for the new mascara.

The thought of that vacation—that travel—had stirred something in her.

6

She knew just what to do to talk herself down from the ledge.

CHAPTER TWO

The sun might've stayed up late during the last weeks of June, but that didn't matter. By the time Diana escaped the office, it was already pitch black save for the plentiful city streetlights. Traffic was lighter, not that it was ever really light in New York.

"Bea?" she called into her hands-free device as she pulled away from House of Phun with her carton of Pad Thai. "I hope it's not too late for me to be calling you?"

"It's lunchtime here, Mom," she said. "I have a few minutes before my next class. What's up?"

Diana never could get her head around the time difference in Japan. "Oh. Good. I was just wondering how you were doing?"

"Oh, great! Fine! There's always something crazy going on here, you know."

"Yeah? Like what?"

"The girls at work took me to an izakaya—that's a bar—in Tokyo where they locked us in a prison cell."

"A prison cell?"

"Yeah, and all the drinks were served in test tubes and beakers with eyeballs floating in it. It was wild. And we were shut in for the night with all these crazy characters chasing after us!"

"Oh. Wow."

"I know, I know, it's not your thing. But it was fun!"

Diana smiled. Her daughter's adventures could fill a very large book. There were so many places she visited, so many new things she learned . . . Diana used to love living vicariously through her daughter, seeing Bea living life to the fullest. But as Bea went on talking a mile-a-minute about how scared she was being chased by a knife-wielding madman during her dinner, a strange feeling pooled in Diana's gut.

It was FOMO. Big time. No, it had never been her dream to be pursued by a murderer, but at least, it was *different*. Diana glanced at her reflection for a moment in the rearview mirror. Since when had she bothered to change her hair style? Not in twenty years. For that long, it had been the same—wake up, go to work, come home, and go to bed only to start it all over again in the morning. She couldn't remember the last time she'd done anything to break routine.

"That sounds so great, honey. I bet—"

"Sorry, Mom. I've got to go. My next class starts in five."

"Okay. I'll see you! Love you!"

"Love you, Mom," Bea said, ending the call.

By the time Diana pulled into the driveway of her Oyster Bay house, it was just before eleven. Outside her front door, the bay was a swath of crystal, sparkling in the moonlight. Yawning, she climbed the stairs to the large colonial's front porch, remembering how homey the house had been before. Back when the kids were young, her mother shared the house, they had a pet golden retriever named Max, and they employed a nanny—every room in the place would be awash in light when she finished the two-hour drive from Manhattan. She'd walk through the door, and Max would bound up to greet her followed by the children, hugging the life out of her. They'd all sit down to dinner and chat about their day, and the kitchen table would be full of laughter and smiles.

Now, the place was cold . . . dark . . . uninviting. Everyone was gone.

When she pushed open the door, she stood in the foyer, remembering how Beatrice and Lily used to screech her name excitedly as they'd grabbed onto the thighs of her pantsuit, nearly toppling her. Max would bark happily, not wanting to be left out.

Now, the grandfather clock struck eleven, and the sound echoed desolately through the empty rooms.

Yes, it had been tiring and frustrating and chaotic before . . . but it had also been nice. *Funny how one never realizes those things until the days are over,* she thought morosely as she kicked off her heels and went to the kitchen. She tried to think of the times she'd had to adjust the thermostat to make it more comfortable for Evan and the other residents. Or helped her kids with homework despite her throbbing migraine. Or made dinner because Jenny, the nanny, wasn't much of a cook. Or taken Max for his walk because no one else wanted to go in the cold.

This is SO much better, she told herself as she unpacked the Thai from the paper bag and poured it all out on the plate. She poured herself

9

a glass of wine and took a sip. *I can have a nice, quiet dinner. No distractions. And I can eat as much as I want, without feeling judged.*

She sat down to eat and twined the noodles around her fork. As she brought it to her mouth, trying to enjoy its spicy-sweet taste, she heard the ticking of the grandfather clock in the foyer. When had that gotten so loud?

Diana opened her phone and turned on some soothing jazz. Better.

More Thai. It really was delicious, a perfect blend of peanuts, sriracha, and brown sugar. She practically inhaled more. Was it sad that this food was, by far, the best part of her day?

Probably.

She took a sip of her wine. *I can also drink as much of this as I want. And likely, I will.*

It made no sense. She and Evan had been on the rocks for over a year. He'd officially filed for divorce months ago. Four months ago, she'd found out he was dating one of Beatrice's old classmates from high school. If there was ever a time to freak out about this arrangement, that would've been it.

And yet she'd been fine. Not a ripple. She'd thrown herself into her work, buried all her emotions.

But now? It was silly, but now she felt unsettled. Now something was gnawing at her gut. Now she felt a crazy desire to break out and do something wild.

And it had all started the second Macey told her about her solo trip to Spain.

"That's because it's your dream, Di," she whispered to herself as she took a gulp of wine. "Well, not Spain. France. But Spain would be nice too. All of it, actually."

Funny. She'd been building up the idea of traveling to Europe in her head all of these years

. . . and yet she was so busy taking care of everyone else, she hadn't even realized it. But it was true. If she closed her eyes now, she could almost taste it like a warm buttered croissant—the historic buildings, the quaint villages, the culture, the food . . .

Grabbing her phone, she tapped on the Instagram app. Maybe she'd see a few pictures, and they wouldn't be as spectacular as she'd pictured it in her head.

Yes. She had so much work to do at Addict. The place needed her. She needed to talk herself down from the ledge and focus on that.

She didn't have much of an Instagram account herself; after all, she had no life. What would she do?—post pictures of her keyboard and her coffee mug? But she liked to follow the girls. This time, she barely looked at a photo of Beatrice in front of some theater in Japan before double-tapping the like. Then she tried entering Macey's name into the search bar, but all she found were a bunch of other Maceys. No Macey who'd recently been to Spain. No sunny vistas and old churches and everything she wanted to see in Europe.

Annoyed, she swiped down to her husband's account, and her jaw fell open.

She checked the name again to make sure she had it right. Yes, he was *ejstjames*.

She stared at the picture again, wishing she could unsee it.

Evan hadn't done anything terribly wrong to her. They'd simply grown apart until even Diana had to admit that, wrapped in their own careers, they'd become virtual strangers living under the same roof. Roommates. The passion, he'd said, was gone, and she had to agree.

She hadn't minded it. She was in her fifth decade of life. She'd figured that if that was as good as it got, she was content. Everything was steady. Predictable. Fine.

But Evan, apparently, *did* mind it—big-time. So much so that he was prepared to make changes that, at this stage of Diana's life, just sounded *exhausting*.

After that speech, six months ago, he'd moved out. Lawyered-up. Started the divorce proceedings. Came by every so often to get his fishing pole, his skis, the things he'd accidentally left during the first sweep. Usually he did so while she was at work, which really was most of the time.

But she didn't hate him. In fact, she missed him. He was a man she'd shared the bulk of her lifetime with, and she loved him. He'd even said that to her, once or twice, too. Maybe it was just out of habit, but he'd often end their calls with "Love you, Di." The one time she'd been there, he'd told her how much he *"missed us."* Even though he'd never suggested getting back together, he'd put a hand on the small of her back and said that he was sorry about the way things had happened, and she was sure there was regret glistening in his eyes.

So she thought it was just a matter of time. This was a late-hitting mid-life crisis. He often entertained whims like that photography kick he went on or that steel pan drum he wanted for his birthday that one year. All that stuff ended up in the closet a couple months later. He just needed the time to work it out of his system.

Of course, it'd been a surprise when she found out he was dating Tilda. Having been in Beatrice's graduating class meant Tilda was almost thirty years Evan's junior. Not only that, Beatrice had always said she had a head like a hot air balloon. Young, beautiful, alluring . . . but nothing upstairs. And Evan was a surgeon . . . top of his class at NYU's School of Medicine . . . used to hobnobbing with the best and the brightest. It wouldn't last. After all, what did they have in common? Eventually, he'd grow bored.

But the photograph that greeted her now was far from boring.

In fact, it was downright scandalous.

It was Evan with his wild salt-and-pepper hair and his tanned, handsome face, wearing a godawful Hawaiian-print shirt, unbuttoned to reveal his graying chest hair and bulging tummy. He was standing in front of a crystal-blue Caribbean Sea with Tilda, who was wearing the tiniest of string bikinis. Their arms were wrapped tightly around each other with Tilda showing off her perfect manicure to the camera . . . and the giant honking eighteen-wheeler headlight of a diamond that made her hand look like a Barbie doll's hand.

Diana just stared at it, sure she was seeing things. *They're in Haiti. We used to go there all the time. Maybe,* she thought stupidly, *it's a joke. Maybe it's a fake she bought from the duty-free store or one of those street vendors.*

Forgetting to breathe, she scanned underneath the photograph to find the caption: *Presenting the soon-to-be new Mrs. St. James! I'm so lucky to have you in my life, babe.*

Diana frowned. *Babe?* Never in her life had he called *her* babe! Maybe because he realized with Tilda, he was completely robbing the cradle. *And the new Mrs. St. James? The divorce isn't final yet. I'm STILL Mrs. St. James, you twit!*

For a second, she thought about commenting that, but decided against it. There were over one hundred comments, all various forms of *Congratulations to the happy couple.* Diana scanned through it, hoping, wishing someone would've commented the obvious: *You're an old man robbing the cradle, and you should act your age.*

No such luck.

She lifted her phone, ready to throw it down and smash it into a million pieces. Her Thai food had gone cold, and now she no longer had the appetite for it.

Then she scrolled back up and caught sight of Evan. The look in his eye was a becoming one. Genuinely happy, the way he hadn't been in a long time with her. He may have been a surgeon, but he wasn't slick or pretentious in the least. No, he was a bit of a bumbler, the kind of guy who was so unassuming and down to earth. It was impossible to hate him.

You poor oblivious, deluded fool, she thought to herself. *I hope she doesn't hurt you.*

But right now, she was the one who was hurting. She poured herself another glass of wine and navigated away from the pictures of people and their happy lives . . . right to the Delta website. She found a flight leaving for Paris in the morning that wasn't too expensive. She added it to her cart and navigated to the checkout.

She hovered her finger over the BUY NOW button, playing a little game of chicken with herself.

Go on. I dare you.

CHAPTER THREE

Stéphane.
Stéphane de Fonblanque.
That was his name.

Actually, it was *Stéphane de Vallier de Fonblanque, duc de Beauville,* if you wanted to get technical about it. He never had been; in fact, the whole nobility thing embarrassed him. He used to roll his eyes every time she'd mock bow before him and ask if he had a ring he wanted her to kiss.

Funny how she remembered that long, unwieldy name, even after all those years.

She sighed with wistfulness at the thought. Talk about a *Sliding Doors* moment—one of those small, seemingly insignificant moments in time that completely changed the trajectory of one's life. For Gwyneth Paltrow, missing a subway train had completely altered her life's direction.

Maybe missing that trip to France when Diana was twenty-two had been *her* moment. The moment when everything veered away from the path she was meant to be on, the one of ultimate happiness and satisfaction. Maybe she'd made a mistake.

After far too much wine, Diana tottered off to bed, lost in her memories. She pulled down the fluffy comforter of the much-too-big king she'd shared with Evan for twenty-eight years and nestled under the covers. Though she knew she could stretch out in the bed any way she liked, she still maintained her small sliver of the right side: her part.

There was that time, when she was a student at NYU working hard to graduate honorably with a dual major in Marketing and Business, when every part of her had been free. Completely unencumbered. Diana had had so many bright and exciting goals for her future, but number one on her list? Travel. Anywhere, really.

Enter Stéphane, who had shaped that dream, given it wings, made the goal more than just a goal. He'd transformed it into a *passion*.

It was his fault she became some enamored with idea of spending an indefinite amount of time meandering about the world, especially Europe. He'd shown up in her Microeconomics class, senior year, on a year-long exchange program. From Nantes, he was descendant of French nobility—his ancestors had served in the court of Louis XIV— and he had that lovely, melodic French accent.

Not to mention, he was brilliant, kind, and adorable with his horn-rimmed glasses and the forever misbehaving cowlick at the very top of his head. He also had the sexiest sideburns, which worked on him. He was used to doing that—going his own way.

She'd been paired with him for the final project but quickly found out that while he was majoring in business, he had the heart of a romantic. They'd spend mere moments on the project, and forever, just talking. He'd tell her, day after day, about different little-known spots around his home—the *Palais de Tokyo, Sainte-Chapelle, Le Marché de Belleville.* He said his favorite thing to do on a rainy afternoon was walk around the many museums, especially *Musée Picasso.* He brought every bit of Paris—the museums, the culture, the architecture—alive for her. But even better than that, he'd read her French poetry— Baudelaire, Rimbaud, Verlaine, and Hugo—and oh, how beautiful it sounded.

She was, for the first time in her life, in love. How could one not hear a beautiful man speak the words *Ne te verrai-je plus que dans l'éternité?, Shall I see you again, only in eternity?* by Baudelaire, and *not* be in love?

"Promise me," he'd said before he left, right at the end of her senior year, a day when she thought she'd die from misery. "Promise me you will come to the ball with me. The Versailles masquerade ball. It is next month, and my family has never missed a ball at the palace since they began having them. These days it is silly. You dress in a period costume and parade around like a peacock for show, but it will be fun. Especially with you there, on my arm. You will make me the proudest peacock of them all."

At that moment, she'd been a puppet on a string. "Yes. Of course," she'd told him. "I'll come."

"For a year," he'd said.

She'd blinked, confused, "For an entire year? Is that how long the ball lasts?"

He'd laughed. "No. The ball is just the start of it. I want you to take the whole year and spend it with me. We'll see all of Europe, starting with Paris. Together. Just the two of us."

"You've seen all of Europe already."

"I have. But it will be different with you."

Then he'd taken her hands in his and whispered in her ear, something she later learned was a line from Hugo: *"Je ne puis demeurer loin de toi plus longtemps."* I cannot stay far from you any longer.

She'd pretty much swooned, and they'd shared a passionate kiss at the airport before he turned and headed to his gate. A few moments later, he turned and announced loudly for the whole concourse to hear: *"Je t'adore, mi amor. We will be together again in Paris!"*

As she watched him walk away, tears in her eyes, she'd promised herself that they would not be far apart for much longer, no matter what she had to do.

That was probably the first—and last—time her life had resembled anything from a movie.

They'd written to each other almost every day; their letters often crossing in the mail.

But then her New York City Dream Job—a marketing manager position at Elizabeth Arden—fell right in her lap.

She hadn't really even been looking. She'd applied on a whim, mostly to keep her parents off her back. But then she'd gotten it and was told she needed to report to work on June 19, which was the same night as the ball.

She'd tried to finagle it. She thought she could go and perhaps start a week later, but her new boss said it was impossible.

It was one of the hardest things she ever had to do, but she wrote to him, declining. She sent him a letter, saying she loved him, but "Maybe I can come out this summer?" He'd responded with great understanding, suggesting they spend a week in Paris, maybe in August.

But then she'd gotten too busy with the job. She was working fourteen-hour days at that time, trying to impress the powers-that-be, and could barely take the time to breathe, much less write a long letter to her boyfriend.

So she'd declined again.

His letters became less and less frequent, more and more detached. *I cannot stay far from you any longer?* Turned out, they *could*. And maybe the next time they saw each other, it *would* be in eternity because months later, she stopped running to the mailbox for them.

She'd met Evan a few months later at an alumni get-together at the college. He was in his first year of med school. Originally, she hadn't been too serious about him. Yes, he was kind and handsome and obviously had a good career ahead of him. But he was no Stéphane; that much was obvious. No man on the continent was.

More things interceded. Her friends told her she was an idiot to treat a pre-med rich, good-looking man like Evan as a placeholder for a silly French pipe dream. Her student loan bill came in, and it was astronomical, making thoughts of travel seem silly when financial disaster was around the corner. Her parents kept reminding her how lucky she was to have found a good job when many recent graduates would've killed to get one, and how she needed to stay in her supervisor's good graces. She simply couldn't tell her employer her intention to traipse off to France a couple months after being hired.

After a while, the letters from Stéphane stopped altogether. He quietly faded into the background, leaving Evan front-and-center.

And the rest was history.

Shivering, she reached into the deep drawer of her night table. Under photo albums and greeting cards, she found it . . . the single letter he'd sent her on rich, creamy stock. It was folded and falling apart at the creases, but when she held it to her nose and inhaled, she remembered the scent of his aftershave, which she imagined she could still smell, even though it had long since disappeared.

She unfolded the letter and pulled her covers up to her chest, remembering Stéphane's warm, heart-melting brown eyes. He could be so boy-next-door one moment, smolderingly romantic the next. And *ooh la la*, that accent! As she read it, she imagined him speaking to her, in that sexy way of his:

My dearest Diana, I can't tell you how much I have missed you in these weeks. With every breath I think of you and await the moment I can have you in my arms again. I feel in my soul that you and I are destined for one another, and I hope you feel the same. Versailles is the home to many treasures, though when you are within its walls, none will be as beautiful or more precious as you. They will pale to you, my love.

He always knew exactly what to say. Never before and never since had she gotten a letter so romantic, so dripping with love and absolute adoration. It made her heart thump wildly, even now, as she read the words.

She had to wonder how different her life would've been if she'd told Elizabeth Arden to get lost. Would she be living in a flat outside of Paris now, the wife of some romantic French aristocrat, living a totally different, exotic life overseas, the envy of all her friends and family?

Maybe.

Maybe she and Stéphane were destined. Maybe there never was supposed to be another lover for either of them. If soul mates did truly exist, then they never truly stopped looking for one another, did they? Maybe, had they married, she and Stéphane would walk the streets of Paris, hand in hand, every day . . . still in love, even now?

Maybe, even after all those interceding years, their love still burned just as hot as before.

Did they even still have that Versailles ball? Head growing fuzzier by the moment from the wine, she grabbed her phone and googled, *Versailles Masquerade Ball.*

A number of results came up. The first one said, *Once a year, around midsummer, you can live like royalty at The Grand Masked Ball in Versailles. Grab your gown and waistcoat, and join us as we relive the opulent masquerade balls and luxurious parties held by the Sun King, Louis XIV in his Palace of Versailles. Yes, THE actual Versailles, the most beautiful and extravagant palace in all the world! Get ready to dance all night—the ball starts at 11:30pm and finishes at dawn! This year's grand event is on June 19! Tickets are on sale now! You don't want to miss the most royal event of the entire year!*

For a moment, she imagined herself being swept across the dance floor of a gilded ballroom by an adorable Frenchman in horn-rimmed glasses, who gazed at her like the only woman in the room and whispered French nothings in her ear.

She sighed. *I've been drinking too much. I have so much going on here. My marketing department can barely breathe without my help. Like I could ever just drop everything and head to France for some silly ball. Especially one that's—*

She studied the date, then looked at her calendar.

Oh . . . only four days away. *That* wouldn't be a problem at all.

18

Then she thought of Evan. They'd weathered a lot of storms together. When all their circle of friends were getting divorced after a couple of years, Diana and Evan had been solid. Unshakeable. Her friends had been jealous, saying, *How do you two make it work so effortlessly?* Through twenty-eight years of wedded bliss, everyone always called them steady. Stable. Not likely to fly off the handle, ruffle feathers, or do anything out of the ordinary.

Boring, really.

But look at Evan now, she thought.

And why shouldn't he? He was a grown adult. What was wrong with being a little reckless and doing the things that would bring him joy? Mid-life crisis or whatever it was called . . . people were allowed to make mistakes. Try new things. It was his life, after all. He didn't need permission from anyone.

And neither do I.

She stared at the photograph on the website of beautiful Versailles with its gorgeous gardens and shimmering fountains, stretching out into the distance, studded with flowers and Roman statues. The white columns of the building itself, in the distance, seemed to go on and on forever out of the range of the camera. It was like something out of a dream. Even when she'd gotten the invitation, she'd never actually imagined being there among those gorgeous gardens and statues, a part of it all.

Why shouldn't I be a little reckless, too?

She was pulled away from her fantasies by a sudden text from Lily, her oldest: *I think somebody's totally lost their marbles!*

Definitely.

Diana was *definitely* no longer in control of her marbles. Really, traveling halfway around the world on a whim to go to a masked ball? What did she think this was, a fairy tale?

She stared at the message, about to respond when another one came through: *Are you going to talk some sense into him?*

Oh. Lily had meant Evan, the wayward husband.

But how did Lily expect her to talk sense into anyone? She wasn't sure she had any of her own left to spare.

And maybe it was time to shake things up a little—just to make life a little more interesting.

CHAPTER FOUR

That morning, Diana did something totally not like her.

Instead of driving into the city early to avoid the traffic, she called and left a message for Sandy, saying something came up and she'd be in later in the afternoon.

Everyone who worked at Addict had the ability to work from home, if they chose. Diana, though, had never taken HR up on the offer. Usually, she enjoyed making the drive, being in the city, and of course, making things happen at work.

But this time, she had no choice.

The thing that had begun tugging at her last night was now yanking her so hard, she could think of nothing else. Certainly not work. A drumbeat kept thrumming in her head: *Europe, Europe, Europe.*

Her eldest, Lily, was twenty-seven and lived with her husband in East Norwich, a town just south. Though they lived not ten minutes apart, Diana's schedule was so busy that they rarely saw one another. Lily didn't seem to mind because she was a chip off the old block—as a realtor, she was constantly hustling all over Long Island, showing homes to prospective buyers. Despite the closeness, theirs was a long-distance relationship—mostly relegated to phone calls and texts. They rarely just "stopped by" unannounced.

That's probably why it took Lily a good ten minutes to answer the door. By then, Diana had been sitting on the porch and pressing the doorbell under the "No Soliciting" placard until her fingertip hurt. Lily came to the door in a bathrobe, her long auburn hair up in a towel turban. Tall and slim with her father's Roman nose and her mother's dramatically arched eyebrows, she moved with all the grace that ten years of ballet lessons and recitals at the Oyster Bay Dance Troupe had given her.

"Mom?" she asked as if she wasn't sure whether aliens had taken over her body. Clutching her robe closed at the neck, she even looked up and down the street for the UFO.

20

"Of course it's me. Can I come in, darling?" Diana asked, motioning.

"Oh. Now I know why you're here. You want to talk about Dad, don't you?" Lily said, clicking her tongue as she pulled open the door and let Diana pass. "Isn't it absolutely gross? I have no idea what's gotten into him."

"Actually, I don't want to talk about him at all," she said, dropping a little care package from Addict's summer lineup on the foyer table. Lily *lived* for her mom's cosmetics. She'd already mailed the same one out to Beatrice in Japan—in the interest of fairness.

She looked around the large foyer, *Better Homes and Gardens*-perfect as usual. It was like her daughter had staged it for a sale—right down to the scent of home-baked cookies wafting through the air.

Not that it would look that way for much longer. She patted her Lily's still-flat stomach. "How are you?"

She gripped her stomach. "You know, everyone is *always* touching my stomach now! It's like I'm not a person. I'm a womb. The peanut's fine. The doctor said everything's normal, so I don't have to go back for another month. It's the size of a pea. I have to get pre-natal vitamins. I keep forgetting to stop by the Rite Aid and—"

Diana shook her head. "That's why I asked how *you* were doing."

Lily shrugged. "Oh, fine. Never better. I was just getting ready to meet a client. The market's booming. I have six showings today. You know that big Victorian on Elm that we thought would never sell? The one with the major HVAC issues? I think I have a potential buyer."

Diana shot her a disapproving *that's still not what I asked* look.

Lily's smile faded, and she yawned. "Okay. Exhausted. And bloated as heck. I feel so funky all the time like my body's been invaded by an alien. You know, I had a bloody nose at the office yesterday that wouldn't stop? It was like a crime scene."

"You? A bloody nose? That's odd. Bea was always the one with the bloody noses."

"I know, right? I've never had anything like that before, but the doctor said all kinds of weird things will be happening to my body now. The other day, I had a weird kink in my back, and I couldn't straighten up for three hours. How did you ever deal with your job and pregnancy? Tell me it gets easier."

Diana sat down at the kitchen nook overlooking the large backyard with cherry trees and a stone patio. It was the perfect family house just

21

like Diana's home had been, right down to the white picket fence. "It does. Your first trimester is always the most exhausting. But after a while you get into that pregnancy glow, and you feel like you can tackle anything. You should probably take it easy now if that's what your body's telling you. You're growing a little human."

She sighed and poured her mother a cup of tea. "I guess."

Knowing Lily, though, she wouldn't. Diana never had; that was for sure. She remembered giving a budget update to the CEO of Addict and twelve members of the board when she was three hours into labor with Bea. It wasn't in their blood to take it easy.

"So tell me. What do you think happened to Dad? I nearly freaked out when I saw that Instagram pic. Did he just flip his lid, or what?"

Diana hitched a shoulder. "Oh, I don't know. In a lot of ways, I think it might make sense."

Lily's bright blue eyes, the same color as Evan's and Bea's, widened. "Make sense! Are you nuts? You know Bea told me my new stepmother-to-be, who, by the way, is *younger* than me, used to be nicknamed "Vidal Sassoon" because all of her brains were in her hair. Aren't you a little grossed out that she's going to be part of the family?"

Diana nodded. "Obviously it's not ideal, but—"

"Ideal? She's a gold digger, pure and simple. Not that Dad has that much gold to be digging." Lily stared at her. "Don't you care at all that he's making this huge mistake?"

"Of course I do. But it's his mistake to make. He's a grown man, dearest, and he knows what he's doing. The divorce is almost final, and the terms have been very amicable. He's doing right by me, which is all I care about. So I have no say in what he does after the papers are signed."

"But . . ." At this point, she looked more like seven than twenty-seven. "Don't you love him anymore?"

"Of course I do."

"Well if you do—you should be warning him he's making a massive mistake! So what if you're not married. You're still friends."

Diana raised her eyes to the ceiling. She'd been through this war—last night in her own head. She didn't want it dragging on anymore. It was too painful.

"Lil. I didn't come to talk to you about your father and what mistakes he may or may not be making. I wanted to tell you something else."

"Uh-oh. That doesn't sound good." Bracing herself, Lily plopped into the seat across from her, not looking at her own cup of tea, which sloshed onto the teacup. "What?"

"Well, I'm thinking of—actually—" She stopped. She wasn't just *thinking* of it any more. Did she want it, or didn't she? Now was the chance to announce it to the world. She took a deep breath. Could she really admit this? *Last chance. A dream in one's own mind is just that. A whim. Nothing. Air. Once you give a voice to it and it's out there in the world, it grows legs. It becomes real.* "I've decided I'm going to take some time off work to do some traveling."

Lily raised an eyebrow. "A vacation? Wow. You? When was the last time you did that?"

"Well, actually, I don't—"

She nodded. "Good. You should. I think if anyone deserves it, you—"

Diana had already begun shaking her head. "No. Not a vacation. More like a sabbatical. A few months. Maybe a year."

Lily paused with her teacup lifted halfway between her chin and the saucer. Her jaw slowly lowered toward the ground. "A . . . year?" Before Diana could answer, the gravity of the suggestion must have finally settled in Lily's brain because she shouted, "Like 365 days? Are you kidding me?"

"No. This has been simmering for a while, and I think it's time. Time for me to get away."

"With who?"

"What do you mean with who?"

"Did you meet someone? Like on Tinder? Because half the time, they can be axe-murderers, and you wouldn't even know based on their pro—"

"I don't even know what a Tinder is. And no, I haven't met anyone. I'm doing it alone. A solo trip. For myself."

Lily's face scrunched up in horror as if Diana had just announced her intention to shave her head and join a cult. "Alone? That's like an invitation to every axe-murderer in every alley you come across!"

"How many axe-murderers do you think are out there?"

"A lot! It's a dangerous world out there! Especially for a woman who's alone. That's what you told me—remember? Remember how you stuffed our stockings with mace and rape whistles every Christmas while we were at college?"

"Yes, but that's—"

"And people really are sick. Most of them have screws loose. Even the normal looking ones. Maybe they don't go around chopping people up with axes, but they do crazy things. Mick told me he had a case come across his desk—a guy kept his own dead mother in his house for twelve years. *Twelve*."

"Your husband is a public defender in one of the most crime-ridden cities in the world. He sees the worst of the worst. I work there, remember? So I'm no Naïve Nancy. And I've survived thus far. I'm fifty-two years old. I can handle myself, dear."

"But . . . but . . ." Lily looked around helplessly. Then she dropped her teacup onto the saucer with a loud clink and grabbed her belly in both hands. "But *this*! Are you seriously going to miss your first grandchild's birth? Aren't you worried about what kind of grandmother that's going to make you?"

That was another word that Diana had not been thrilled with. Evan was dating Miss Teen USA and living the life of a young, freewheeling bachelor, and here she was—eight months from being a knitting, cookie-baking grandma with gray hair and bifocals. It hadn't seemed fair. "Of course not! I have plenty of money to fly back for the birth," she said.

"But what if I can't get in touch with you? What if you're somewhere in Switzerland—I don't know—yodeling on a mountainside, and there are no phones nearby?" She clapped her hands to her cheeks like the kid in *Home Alone*. "The baby's due in December. I can't believe you're seriously considering this. Where would you go?"

"Paris," she said immediately, grabbing her phone and navigating to the page for the ball. "I've always wanted to see Versailles, you know. The Palace of Louis XVI?"

"Of course I know Versailles. It's great and all, but . . . Okay. Then go for a week. You don't have to move in, do you? I mean, really!"

"That's just to start. I want to see so many things in Europe. Florence . . . Austria . . . I made a list. I think it'd be an adventure."

"Adventure? You hate adventure!"

"Well . . . I don't think so. I don't know. I've never really been on one."

"You hate it. Trust me. That's why you planned our Disney vacations to the minute. Remember? *Nine twenty-five: Wait on line for It's a Small World. Nine thirty-five: Go on It's a Small World. Nine Forty-seven: Get off It's a Small World—Bathroom break?*"

Diana stayed silent. *Touché.*

"Do you even have a valid passport?"

"Of course. I had to get one for work." She had one, yes, but had she used it? No. Though she'd dutifully renewed it every ten years, she'd never put very many stamps in it. In fact, the only ones she had were from her trips to Haiti.

Lily had risen to her feet and was now pacing the hardwood floors at furious clip, arms akimbo. "What about your house? You're just going to leave it empty for a whole year? Who's going to take care of it?"

"I thought I'd get you to rent it out for me. I can do that, right? You could find someone who wants to rent it?"

"Well, yes, in a heartbeat . . ." Lily admitted, clearly not wanting anything to do with it. It made sense. She'd grown up there. The thought of someone using her bedroom as their exercise room, sweating all over her pink carpets, probably wasn't very pleasant. "And work? They worship you there. The place would probably self-destruct if you missed a day. You really think they'll be okay with this?"

"I haven't told Alina yet. But I've been working there forever. They owe me this for my loyalty. Besides, Phil can fill in for me. They do give sabbaticals to their top employees. Last year, someone in accounting went on a pilgrimage to Mecca for over six months."

"Okay, but that was to have a religious experience," Lily said. "What are you hoping to achieve? Some sort of enlightenment? You have so much right here. A house most people would kill for—right on the bay. A great job. A great *life.*"

Diana sat there, listening to the laundry list of things she should be thankful for and feeling a little numb. It was that overarching feeling of loneliness that had settled over her last night that she couldn't shake. Was this all? For the rest of her life? Day after day of the same drudgery, pressing through life alone and wondering *what if?* "Honestly," she admitted softly. "I'm just not happy."

Lily's lips twisted. "You?"

Diana almost laughed. Yes, it was the first time she'd admitted it aloud. But it was almost as if her daughter had never considered her mother's happiness before. As if she was just supposed to be content with her life, no matter what. "Yes, me."

"Is this because of Dad? I know what he did was terrible, but—"

"It has nothing to do with your father. It's about me. For once. Looking out for myself for the first time, instead of everyone else."

At first, Diana thought her daughter understood. That she'd be on board. Instead, she let out a cry of frustration.

"Oh, my god," Lily whispered, grabbing her own phone and stabbing something in. "Oh. My. God. I just can't believe I'm hearing this right. And here I thought you were the *sane* parent in the family! Did you and Dad actually time your mid-life crises to coordinate like this?"

"What are you doing?" Diana asked, shifting in her seat.

She continued to poke at her phone display in a rather angry way. "Calling Bea. Maybe she can talk you down from the ledge you're about to dive from—face-first."

Diana nodded. That was just fine. Bea was the free spirit. The traveler. The wanderlust. She was the one who took time off during school to see the world, finally landing herself in Japan and finishing her Masters overseas. If anyone would be on board with these plans, it was her kooky, lovable youngest daughter.

Lily set the phone down on the kitchen table on speaker as it rang. A second later, someone picked up, and the sound of chattering crowds and a throbbing bass filled the room. "Can't talk, Lil. I'm out with Hai."

Hai was Bea's boyfriend of the past eight months, and another English teacher at the school she taught at in Japan. He was a native Japanese who'd spent most of his childhood in California and had shown her around when she first arrived. Supposedly, it was serious. Diana checked her watch. It was probably near midnight there.

"No, you have to talk! This is important!" Lily shouted over the roar, banging her fists on the table. The phone slipped, and Lily propped it up again. "We're having a crisis here! Listen, I've got Mom here, and you're never going to believe—"

"I know. I know already, Lil. I saw he's marrying Vidal. Crazy old coot. That's why I'm out here on a school night. Hai's getting me loaded up on *nihonshu*."

26

"What?" Lily asked, confused.

"Sake."

"Oh." Lily glared at Diana. "Well, have one for me too. But that's not all. You might want to do another shot when you hear what Mom's got to tell us."

Diana shushed her. The last thing she wanted was her youngest getting loaded in some strange country, even with the boyfriend she supposedly trusted.

A pause. Then Bea said, "Oh, god. What, Mom? Are you pregnant, too?"

Diana let out the breath she'd been holding in shock. "Very funny. Nothing like that. It's not even that big a deal. It really has very little bearing on either of you."

"Well, what?"

This time, Diana didn't mind spilling her plans. She'd never really seen eye-to-eye with her youngest because she was so whimsical and prone to flights of fancy, but now she felt like a kindred spirit. It'd be nice to have someone on her side, telling Lily that this was a good plan.

"I'm just going to take a year off from my job and do a little traveling. To Europe."

A longer pause. Some crazy Japanese pop song came on in the background. Then Bea said, "You, Mom? Really? Hold on." She shouted something in Japanese to someone else in the room. "I'm back. Mom, you're traveling? Are you sure?"

It was as if Diana had announced she wanted to feed herself to a pit of rabid wolves. "What is that supposed to mean?"

"I mean, why would you even do that? Isn't that kind of out of left field? You have so much right at home. A good career. Family. Nice house."

"Right?" Lily slapped the table with her palm. "That's just what I said."

Diana stared at the phone and at her eldest daughter. She'd carried them and raised them, and this was the thanks she got? Them ganging up on her? Why weren't they reading Evan the riot act too? It wasn't as if she'd just announced her plans to marry someone half her age . . . all she wanted to do was take a year off. "Bea, I thought you, of all people, would understand."

"I understand wanting to experience life. But you've never wanted to do this before. You had your job. Your family. Your friends. Your house. You never struck me as the type to want to say goodbye to all that. And besides, you plan things like crazy. Remember that Disney debac—"

"Truthfully, I'm not happy," Diana stated bluntly.

The room dissolved into silence. Even the crowded Japanese barroom seemed to hush up. Lily said, "You said that before. But do you think this'll make you happy?"

Diana shrugged, "I don't know. I just know I need to do something different. Before I'm too old to do anything."

"Mom, you're not eighty," Lily sighed.

"But I'm not twenty anymore, either."

"Well, if different is all you want, maybe you should dye your hair blonde." When Diana continued to shake her head, Bea added, "You're just freaked out over Dad sowing his wild oats, and now you think you have to, too. That's what this is. If you can't beat 'em, join 'em."

"No, it's—"

Lily nodded, "Yeah. Definitely." She checked the time on her phone. "Look, I've got to go. I have a meeting at eleven. Mom, why don't you take a few weeks and think it over? Then you can make the decision with a clear head, not influenced by Dad and—"

"I can't do that," Diana said immediately.

"Why not?" the girls asked in unison.

"Well," she said, grabbing her phone and navigating to the website of the ball. "I've always wanted to go to this. And if I'm going to get there, I need to move right away."

She passed it over to Lily to look at. "What is it?" Bea whined like the nagging little sister.

"It's a ball," Lily said, her nose scrunched in confusion. "A masquerade ball at Versailles, where they dress up in old period costumes and dance all night. Oh, my gosh, talk about cheese. Really?"

"A what?" Bea blurted. "Why? You mean like . . . a real ball? I didn't even know they had those anymore."

Now, it was as if she'd announced she wanted to audition for clown school. Diana snatched the phone back. This was not the time to tell them about Stéphane and her dreams that he'd be there after all this time. That was for sure. They'd laugh at her. "I don't know. It sounds fun. I'd really like to go to it. Just once in my life. That's all."

"Oh, my god, Mom!" Lily said in disbelief. "Now you *really* must be pulling our legs. I mean, how could you even possibly do that? That ball is four days away!"

"I can do it," Diana said firmly. "I'm sure of it."

"You can move your stuff out of the house and get it ready to rent? And work is going to be okay with you taking off at the end of the week? For a whole year? You're really going to jet off like that on them and leave them without properly training your replacement? Really?"

Bea laughed. "Seriously!" she said in agreement.

There they were, ganging up on her again. Her own flesh and blood. She'd always supported them in their dreams . . . was it too much to ask for a little support in hers?

Diana rose to her feet and placed her palms on the table. "Now listen here, girls. I've lived my whole live for you. I've rearranged my life and my finances for your school trips, your activities, your education . . . I went through the pain of childbirth for you. And now— I'm doing this for me. With or without your approval," she said, sticking her chin up high. "And you can bet your life . . . even if it kills me . . . I am making it to that ball!"

A long silence prevailed after that monologue. One that seemed to stretch on forever, making Diana wonder if they were even on her side at all. Didn't they want her to be happy?

"Well, you're a grown woman," Bea finally said. "If that's what you want . . ."

Lily nodded, "Yep. I guess we can't stop you. And I'm sure you'll love it there. I know I've always wanted to go to Paris too."

She even managed a smile.

Diana considered that a win. Now, all she had to do was tell her supervisor at work, and soon she'd be free. What could go wrong?

CHAPTER FIVE

"I'm sorry, but have you lost your mind?"

Diana stood in front of Alina Myers, the white-haired beautiful magazine-cover-worthy CEO of Addict. Only thirty herself when she started the corporation, she'd snapped Diana up from Elizabeth Arden as her right-hand girl when the brand was only a fledgling operation with one small warehouse in Cranbury, New Jersey. After all these years, Diana had come to see her not only as a mentor but as a friend.

Diana smiled as she looked past her at the skyscraper across the street. As her right hand, Diana had the office next to Alina's with just as nice a view. Yes, Addict had been good to her. But she'd been good to it too. Loyal and indispensable. A rock. She'd built this company to the success it was. She had nurtured it and given it what it needed to grow.

And now, she needed this.

"I know, it sounds crazy. But I've been batting the sabbatical idea around for a long time." *Well, really for only a day . . . to be honest. But when it's right, it's right!* "And I'm ready to take it. I do feel like the company will be in good hands with Phil."

"Yes, I agree," Alina said, almost too readily, tapping her gold-accented pen on the pad in front of her. "But . . . we're right in the middle of finishing up the fall line. Can't you give me a little bit of a notice? We can plan your last day for the fall."

She shook her head. "Unfortunately, I have a bit of a schedule to—"

"All right. When did you want your last day to be?"

"Well . . . tomorrow."

Rarely was Alina Myers struck speechless, but she was nearly there now. She practically choked on her gasp of surprise. "Tomorrow?"

"Yes." If Alina was looking at her like she'd suddenly sprouted wings and horns now, the whole *I need to make it to the ball, Cinderella-thing*, probably wouldn't go over much better. So she fudged it. "Yes. There's a little scheduling issue that . . ."

She stopped when Alina held up a manicured hand. "That's altogether unacceptable, Diana. You have to understand. There's paperwork to fill out. Plans that need to be made. You've served me well for over twenty years, but as much as I'd like to grant that to you, it's really putting me in a hard spot."

"In twenty years, have I ever asked you for anything?" Diana asked.

Alina sat up behind the massive desk and closed her silk blazer over her camisole. She shook her head. "No, Diana, you've been a model employee, and I'm as grateful as anyone can be. But if I make concessions for you, I'll have to make them for everyone else. For Phil, whenever he wants to go to Vegas and blow his life's savings. For the others, for every little whim they have. You're talking about an entire year here, Diana. That's going to affect the business in big ways. Big ways."

"But Phil—"

"Phil doesn't have the insight you have. For him, it's a job. For you, it was your *life*."

"I know." That was true. It *was* her life. For so long, it was everything she thought about, besides her family. Sometimes, she hated to admit, *instead* of her family. And what had it gotten her? She had money, *lots* of money in the bank, socked away for a comfortable retirement, but she'd never had the time to enjoy it. Not in the way she really wanted to.

Now, she could feel that opportunity slipping away . . .

She took a deep breath and said, "I'm sorry you feel that way, Alina. If that's your final decision, then I'll have to tender my resignation."

Alina's eyes bulged, "Diana. Are you sure? Think about what you're doing. Giving everything up. For what?"

"I have been thinking. And that's the problem. I've been thinking about things for so long. Wanting them. But thinking without action is worthless. And I'm fifty-two years old. I have the means to travel the world. Why am I waiting to enjoy my life?"

Alina pushed back from her desk. She looked like she was about to say something about how it was a mistake, but then she stopped. "Di. You're making a huge mistake. This company is your life. You can't just leave it."

"I can. I think I already just quit."

31

"Diana. Be serious. You can't. Why don't you take a vacation? You have weeks and weeks of vacation time banked. Take the month of July if you feel you must."

She shook her head. If she was going to do this, she was going to do it all-in. Not with the worry of everything she was missing at work hanging over her head. That would only compel her to check her work email every few minutes and ruin the purpose of the trip. Which was, like Macey had said, *Clearing her mind.*

"I don't think so. But I appreciate everything you've done for me," Diana said, then walked out the door, her legs feeling strangely wooden.

Had that really happened? Had she just quit her job? The thing that had been Priority Number One in her life for thirty years?

She expected to feel lost like a plastic bag drifting on a gust of wind. But suddenly, her shoulders lifted, and a sense of calm fell over her. With all the worries of work behind her, she found she really didn't have much else on her to-do list at all. Just:

Dealing with the house
Making travel plans
Packing

As she opened the door to her office, she said to Sandy, "Could you get my daughter Lily on the phone? Thanks."

"Sure . . ." Sandy said, hand on the phone, confusion on her face. "What's wrong?"

"Nothing!" Diana said, and then she realized what it was. She was smiling from ear to ear, like a crazy person on her way to the nuthouse. Had she ever been this happy at work before?

She closed the door behind her, sat down in her chair, and for the first time, didn't bother to look at the urgent emails piling up in her inbox. Instead, she pulled away from the desk and did a few spins in her executive chair, like she was on a carousel, feeling light—relieved—like a kid again.

It was almost the same giddy feeling she'd had when she was in love with Stéphane.

Yes, I knew this was right! she thought to herself as the phone buzzed and Sandy said, "Lily St. James-Brandt on the line."

"Thanks, Sandy!" she said, leaning forward as the click came. "Lil?"

"Hi, Mom. I'm thinking you're calling me because you have more news that's bound to give me a heart attack. Am I right?"

Diana laughed. "Well, I—"

"I talked it over with Mick an hour ago. He thinks you're bonkers."

"Well, great, tell my son-in-law thanks very much for his opinion," she said matter-of-factly. Mick was all right, even for a lawyer, and he loved Lily. So that was all that mattered. He'd be a good father to their child. "Anyway, I decided about renting out the house, and I do need your help with that."

"Ugh," Lily sighed. "So you're going through with it. Really? Are you sure you don't want to—"

"I just quit my job," she blurted. Yes, saying it out loud made it all the more real. "Lily. I'm doing this. There's no talking me out of it now."

There was a long pause. "Oh, my god. Seriously?" It was in the same tone she would've used if Diana had announced she had three months to live.

"Really. I feel great."

"That makes one of us."

"Stop being so dramatic! I'm happy about it. Ecstatic. You should be too. I can't wait."

"You can be ecstatic. What I'm less than ecstatic about is the thought of someone messing up my childhood bedroom beyond repair. What do you want to do with all your furniture?"

"Oh, just rent it, furnished. I'll get a PODS container for the stuff we want to store. Maybe Mick can help move it for me?"

"I'm sure he could. But are you sure? You have no idea what renters have been known to do. The last place I rented out—a guy used to fix motorcycles in the living room and dripped oil and grease all over the hardwood floors. I'm not sure I want that same guy sleeping on my mattress!"

"*You* don't sleep on it anymore. No one has. No one has actually gone in your room in about six years. Your father wanted to turn your room into a man cave for his hobbies, but he never had the chance. It's a shrine to Lily St. James, complete with all your American Girl dolls that you can come and retrieve any day you'd like. And anyway, I'm sure you'll vet potential tenants properly. You think people will be interested?"

"Oh, yes. Everyone will be interested. I put feelers out and got a whole bunch of bites. Almost ninety. But no one I'd approve of," she said sourly. "We'll need someone who's going to care for it like . . . well, like you did."

Diana smiled. Of course Lily had already put out feelers. She was proactive, always preparing for the worst eventuality instead of letting the chips fall where they may. That was something *Diana* would've done.

"Mom, still . . . I have to ask. Are you sure about this?" Her daughter's voice cracked with emotion. That was Lily, the responsible, sensitive one. Any change from the status quo shattered her. She was so much like Diana that it was uncanny. Maybe Diana had raised her that way. Maybe she should've been teaching her to be more go-with-the-flow.

"Honey. I promise. I'll be there for the baby."

"It's not that. It's just that . . . I mean . . . Dad, I expected this kind of thing from. But you? You've never done anything crazy like this, and it's scaring me. Are you okay? I just . . . don't want to see you do something you'll regret."

"I'm fine, darling," Diana said, throwing some of her things into a box and getting ready to jet out of the building for the very last time in her career. She felt like she was thinking clearly for the first time in her life. Sure, the doubts were there, but there really was nothing that she would regret now. She'd made the career she wanted and followed this path to its end. Now was time for a new journey.

Besides, she'd already spent enough time regretting.

Now was the time to make up for those lost dreams.

"Just find a renter for the house—for me. Anyone. I trust you," she said to Lily, pulling up the website for Versailles again. There were so many rooms, so many treasures, so many secrets to explore, and if she just took the risk, she'd be there soon, experiencing it all. "I've got to go. I have an adventure to plan."

CHAPTER SIX

"And . . . done!" Diana said, pressing the BUY NOW button on the airline website.

It was a far cry from the waffling she'd done the day before. This time, there was no hesitation. No refunds or exchanges. Nothing short of an act of nature would get her to turn back now. She was finally doing this!

She was now the official owner of a one-way first-class ticket to Paris leaving the following evening from JFK. A seven-hour nonstop flight arriving at Charles de Gaulle Airport early the next morning. The red-eye—but she didn't think it was possible to be anymore awake.

She found an inn off the beaten path, though still with a view of the Eiffel Tower, of course. After booking a suite, she navigated over to the website for Versailles and found the page for the masked ball. The price for a VIP ticket, including a buffet dinner, was 183 euros. She did the mental math in her head. Two and a quarter hundred in dollars. Plus, she'd have to rent a baroque costume, shoes, and jewelry, something that could be done right at the palace, though it looked expensive for one night of fun.

But it was a small price to pay for fulfilling the dream of a lifetime. This would be an experience she'd never forget. She added the single ticket to her cart and checked out without a second's thought, humming a little tune as she typed in her address.

I am really doing this. In twenty-four hours, I will have said goodbye to New York, goodbye to America . . . for a full year! A thrill passed through her as she entered her credit card digits.

With her tickets booked, she decided she'd finish her packing tomorrow. Most of her personal things were already in boxes, waiting to go into the POD that was being delivered tomorrow morning. Mick and Lily would help load stuff up, so she could say goodbye to them that afternoon. She had one small suitcase, deciding that anything she forgot, she could always purchase when she got there. Paris might have a *little* bit of a shopping district, or so she'd heard?

She giggled at the thought. Addict made great fragrances, but nothing beat honest-to-goodness actual French perfume. She couldn't wait to go sample it all. And the food? And the culture? Soon, she'd be swimming in it!

She sat down in her comfortable chair, took a sip of wine, and rubbed her hands together. Nearly thirty years in business had told her one thing: never operate without a plan. Now was the time to come up with her itinerary. *No,* she wasn't as ridiculous as her kids said she was. Disney had been fun, regardless of whatever they remembered. This plan would be easy, customizable, manageable . . . and would allow her to see all of the hundreds of things she couldn't wait to see.

She spread out a map, her laptop, and a notebook in front of her. At the top, she wrote:

June 20: Arrival at Charles de Gaulle 8 AM

Then she wrote:

8:15 AM – Get Luggage
8:45 AM Take Cab to Inn

She did a little googling to find out how long it would take the cab to get her to the inn. Thirty-six minutes without traffic. Allowing a few minutes for traffic, she wrote in the next item on her agenda:

9:30 AM Check into Inn
10 AM Stop at Café de Flore for a pastry

The place was absolutely adorable, according to the website. And they had a *mille-feuille* which looked absolutely delectable. She wrote, *Mille-feuille???* And circled it. Then:

11 AM Take cab to the Louvre . . .

She crossed that out. Maybe instead, she should go to the Picasso Museum first, since that was Stéphane's favorite place. Or both? Two hours should be enough for both of them, if she just caught the major pieces of art. Then she could grab a late lunch at . . .

She quickly googled cafes close to the art museum for lunch. Checking their menus, she settled on a little bistro down the street and wrote down, *Salade de queues d'écrevisses au jambon de canard,* because whatever it was . . . it looked quite scrumptious on the website.

After that, she googled how far the Arc de Triomphe was from the restaurant. She would allow herself an hour for lunch and fifteen minutes to take pictures of herself in front of the Arc. Maybe she'd post one or two on her empty Instagram, just to let Evan know that her life was going on just fine without him.

After that, she would have plenty of time to get to the top of the Eiffel Tower before sundown, take pictures of it as it lit up for night, and maybe return to the hotel for dinner.

Perfect. Since the ball wasn't until later the next evening, she could spend the entire next day visiting those lesser-known Parisian sights Stéphane had told her about.

As she stared at the map, she frowned. No, wait. *Before* going to the Arc, she'd *have* to stop by Notre Dame Cathedral since it was in an entirely different direction. And the Pantheon? What about the *Sacré Cœur? Les Invalides?* And did that bridge, *Pont des Arts,* still have all the locks? Stéphane had said he wanted to put one there for her, but last she heard, the locks were causing structural damage to the bridge.

And on and on. She planned everything to the moment, just as if she'd been scheduling one of her meetings. She got on such a roll with it that she outlined almost the first full month of her travels. After a few days in that inn, seeing all the sights around Paris, she'd have to rent a car so that she could move on to Nantes. She looked up and entered in the car rental information so she could call about that. Then she'd go along the coast . . . to LaRochelle . . . Toulouse . . . a stop in Barcelona to say she'd been to Spain, before heading to Nice and the French Riviera. Then, of course, on to Florence!

At that moment, she tapped her chin, wondering if she should try to book the hotels now. No, probably not. As good as her itinerary was, there was always the chance something could throw it off a bit. Better to book the hotels as she went. They'd likely have a vacancy.

It didn't sit right with her—not having an exact date and destination. Thinking more on it, though, she decided to write in exactly *when* she should call each hotel and make the reservation so she wouldn't forget. She found all the nicest hotels in the area, and wrote down their phone numbers.

Before long, though, she had filled the entire notebook with sights she wanted to see—all the usual places that anyone taking a first trip to Europe would want to visit. There were dozens more ideas she had, but she had to keep this realistic. She did a couple iterations of the itinerary until there were balls of crumpled paper all around her, but eventually, she was satisfied.

As she put on the finishing touches, her phone buzzed with a text.

She looked at the display. Sure enough, it was from the man who had forgotten he was still married to her. *Lily called. She said she's worried about you.*

So look at that, he hadn't forgotten her after all. Of course, he remembered her just long enough to chastise her.

Diana rolled her eyes, picked up the phone, and dialed his number. The last thing she wanted to do was to hear his voice when she was trying to look toward the future, but she had no choice. Always one to be attached to his cell, he answered immediately. "Diana, love, are you all right?"

"I am. But should I first say congratulations?" She tried not to choke on the word. She didn't want to make it seem like she'd been trolling his Instagram, so she added, "The kids told me. I should probably take this moment to remind you, though, that I haven't signed anything to make the divorce official."

"Ah, yes. My attorney says the papers should be on your doorstep Monday, at the latest."

"Oh. Well, I won't be here. Did you think at all you might be jumping the gun by announcing the engagement before all the i's were dotted?"

He laughed in that goofy way that made it hard to hate him. "I agree. But Tilly always wanted a summer wedding. And her parents have this whole plan for August. The whole nine yards. Half the state will be there."

But I won't. Thank God. "I see. That sounds lovely. But I seem to remember you wanting a small wedding, which was why you and I got married upstate."

He chuckled. "Well, I figure, you only live once. Lily told me about the big trip. Are you sure that's wise, love?"

"Yes, I am."

"And is it true you quit your job?"

"Yes, I did."

"You loved that job."

"Yes, I did."

"And Lily says you told her to find some strangers to rent out the house. You loved that place like it was one of your kids, you know. None of this is like you."

"Evan, we haven't been living under the same roof for over a year. Before then, you were the one who said we were acting like

38

roommates, that we'd lost our connection," she said with a sigh. "I thought you'd understand . . . you don't know what I'm like at all."

"Perhaps that's true. And I'm sorry about that."

Was that pity in his voice? "I'm not. I agree with that. And the feeling's mutual. Until your Instagram post, I thought Vi—I mean, Tilda—was just a whim. I hadn't realized it was serious."

"Yes. Well, that's like me, isn't it? But it's not *you*. And I do know that you're not the type to go off on whims," he said, and she could hear the smile in his voice. "That's always been my department. Love, you needed a schedule just to do your Christmas shopping. Didn't you? You'd be lost without that planner of yours."

She frowned. "Well—"

"And all those lovely beach vacations we took, remember, to Haiti? The ones where we could just go with the flow? You had an agenda. Disney was a death march. Admit it."

Her frown deepened. She'd thought they'd had fun, though it was a little hectic, but apparently, no one else in the family had. He'd never complained about it before. In fact, he'd *praised* her for being so organized and allowing them to see and do as much as possible on their vacation. So what if it wasn't relaxing? Where was this hostility coming from?

Oh, probably "Tilly." His new fiancé was likely loose and free as the summer wind. How *wonderful* of her. They were just too peas in a pod, made for each other.

But that's what happened when one's head was the equivalent of a wind tunnel.

"What does it matter to you, Evan, what I do on this trip? This is no business of yours," she said, trying to keep her voice aloof, unstrained.

"It is if it affects the children. And Lily . . . you know her. She gets anxious about things. She hates the things she can't control because she takes after you. She called me this morning, all distraught. She's worrying about you. And you know that isn't good for her or the baby."

And you really think finding out the stepmother is younger than she is has no impact on her mental health? Diana sighed. "Why is it that in our family, some people get to do whatever they want. And yet there are so many restrictions on me?"

"You can do what you like, of course, love," he assured her. "I just wonder if you're upset about something, and making a rash mistake."

"Now, Evan, what on earth do I have to be upset about? I'm perfectly happy. You have to remember when we first met . . . Paris was all I ever talked about."

"I remember. But a *year?* Are you sure you can—"

"I wanted to go. But we never did. Why is that?"

"Because Paris is nasty and ugly. You forget, I was there in Europe once before I met you."

"I don't forget that. You would tell me about it, every time I suggested we take a trip

ther—"

"It's true! It is nothing like they say on TV. You have this dream of it. Of this beautiful, romantic city of sparkling light. But I promise, nothing will live up to that. And you're going to be disappointed."

She'd stopped listening to him by then. "I don't care," she said bluntly. "At least I will have been there and can cross it off my bucket list. Did you call for a reason? Or were you just calling to wish me bon voyage?"

"*Bon voyage,*" he said. "Of course, love, I want you to have a wonderful time. Send me a postcard, eh?"

"Good. I'll give you the address of the hotel I'm staying at if you'd like to have the papers sent there," she said. "I don't want to delay your wedding plans."

"Thank you, love."

"Evan, I've got to go. I have a plane to catch."

She ended the call and looked down at her itinerary. Of course, plans were a good thing. The last thing she needed in her life was to have someone like Evan, filling her with doubts, trying to get her sidetracked. Nothing could hold her back now. She was finally on her way.

CHAPTER SEVEN

That evening, after kissing Lily and Mick goodbye, Diana arrived at JFK airport with plenty of time to spare before her flight. When the flight attendant announced that the first-class passengers could now begin boarding, a thrill of excitement passed through her. Cradling her jacket and neck pillow in her arms, wearing a black wrinkle-free travel suit she'd picked up at Saks, she took a long look at the lights of New York City before boarding the plane.

If all goes well, you're not going to see those lights for a very long time.

Oh, stop it, Diana! Everything is going to go well. It's your dream. Don't listen to the nay-sayers! It's going to be amazing!

Smiling, she navigated to the leather seats in first class and squeezed into the one near the window. As she made herself comfortable, the flight attendant offered her a drink. "Just some water," she said, taking out the book she was reading and getting settled. "Thanks."

As she grabbed her phone to silence it, she noticed she had a text.

It was from Evan. *Have a good trip, love. Give me that address when you can.*

She frowned, then typed in very bluntly: *Le Bonne Auberge, rue de Charonne.*

Then she sighed. If all he cared about was getting her precious signature on the papers that would effectively dissolve everything that had ever existed between them, she wasn't going to waste one more second thinking of him.

She peered out the oval window. Past the busy runway full of planes taking off and arriving, she could just make out the tops of the buildings in the city. Somewhere out there was the business she'd helped build. She was saying goodbye to her stability, to the town she had been born and lived her whole life in, to everything she'd ever known.

Oh, don't be dramatic. You'll be back. Happier. And think of all the stories you'll have!

She opened her book to start reading as the rest of the passengers filtered into the cabin, but then closed it on her lap. She was too excited, imagining those stories. Maybe she'd meet Stéphane again. Wouldn't that be crazy after nearly thirty years? Well, not so crazy . . . he'd said his family always went every year to the ball at Versailles. Maybe he'd be there.

A thrill passed through her. She had thought of googling him a thousand times and usually resisted. After all, a man like him was perfect. He probably had a perfect wife now, a great job, a life that was fulfilling and wonderful, even without her. He probably didn't even remember her. He was likely friends with the prime minister and the president, running around in fabulous circles, fully embracing his nobility like he never had before. In a moment of weakness, she had put his name in the search bar once, but very little had come up, and she hadn't bothered to dig more. He'd said his family was intensely private.

But maybe, just maybe . . .

At that moment, she slipped into a fantasy. Diana—walking the magnificent gardens of Versailles in a bright yellow ball gown with flowing skirts, a la Belle in *Beauty and the Beast*. Her dark hair piled very romantically on her head in curls. The dark sky glittering with stars. As she walked to the balustrade and looked out over the fountains and sculptures, she'd see him there, among the guests. Yes, he'd be older with crow's feet and salt-and-pepper hair, but he'd have aged like Sean Connery—getting better looking over the years.

The moment their eyes would connect, electricity would zap through the air. He'd swerve around the others to be by her side. "Diana," he'd say breathlessly in that yummy French accent, taking her hand and pressing a chaste kiss onto the top of it, "I have waited thirty years for you. I've never forgotten you, *mon amour*." Then he'd recite some ridiculously romantic poem from Baudelaire, and she'd melt into a pile of goo at his feet.

And they'd live happily ever after in some remote chateau overlooking a lake and with a view of the Eiffel Tower in the distance. Of course.

It had been a long time since she'd indulged in fairy tale fantasies like that. But, of course, at Versailles with Stéphane, she wouldn't be able to help it. The atmosphere would be so perfect. It was, like he had said . . . *destiny.*

"I'm so sorry," a voice suddenly said in a deep French accent, stirring her from her reverie.

She looked up at the woman next to her, who was busy trying to stuff a large carry-on under her seat. The woman was probably around Diana's age, though a bit heavier, but well-put together, wearing heavy makeup and bright red lipstick. Her hair was up in a psychedelic-patterned scarf, and she smelled heavily of Chanel No. 5. The woman pointed a long manicured fingernail at the ground, and Diana followed it to realize that the book had slipped from her lap and was now lying, spine-up, on the ground.

Diana reached down and picked it up. Had the woman knocked it off? She'd been so completely taken away by her fantasy that she hadn't noticed.

"No problem," she said with a smile as the woman sat down in her chair and heaved a large sigh. "Returning to France from vacation?"

"An extended one, I suppose," the woman said. "I was traveling North America for the past three months. I always wanted to see it, so I decided to take a trip by myself since my husband wasn't interested. I did Hollywood, then Las Vegas, Chicago, Florida, and New York. All the big places."

Diana smiled brightly. How fortuitous this was that, on the eve of flying out to France, she finds someone who is just returning from her own voyage of self-discovery? *See, Diana. People do it, have a great time, and survive with amazing stories of adventure to last the rest of their lives!*

"Oh? That's amazing. So how did you—"

"It was awful," the woman groaned. "Simply terrible. I cannot wait to be home and wake from this horrific nightmare."

Diana paused, dumbfounded. "Oh. It was that bad?"

"Worse," she said with a deep frown, shuddering at the memory. "In fact, the *worst*. The food was terrible. The hotels were atrocious. The landmarks are dirty and dinky and unimpressive. Vegas was full of dirt! The Grand Canyon is a hole! I was mugged in Chicago. It rained all the time. Everything paled to my imagination. I had been dreaming of this my entire life. And it was nothing like what I expected. I only stayed on my itinerary, hoping everything would get better. It never did. That is why I am cutting my trip short. I had planned to go on to Boston, but no more. I'm done."

"That . . ." Diana trailed off. *Sounds like me. Dreaming, my whole life. Only to . . .*

Only to what? To learn that everything Evan had warned her about Europe was the truth, and that she'd inflated her dreams of this trip to some fantasy world that no place on earth could ever live up to?

Her heart skipped a beat as she thought of what Evan had said. The last thing she wanted to do was to go on this trip and prove Evan right. "That's awful."

The woman nodded, "Yes. I'd wanted so much from this trip since I planned it for so long. Built it up in my head, and I suppose that was a mistake. Oh. Well. At least I am going home. Are you on vacation?"

Diana smiled weakly. "Um. Yes. A small one," she lied. "It will be my first time in Paris. Maybe you can give me some suggestions as far as places to visit?" she asked, though she didn't really want to hear any more ideas that could mess with her carefully plotted itinerary.

The plane doors closed. The flight attendants began to give their safety demonstrations, and the plane began to taxi away from the gate. Diana really didn't want to spend seven hours listening to a woman complain about how awful her trip was, but she wasn't sure she had a choice. It was too late to turn back now.

Luckily, as soon as the plane began to power down the runway, the woman fell asleep, snoring loudly.

That was okay. Everyone was entitled to their own opinion. She happened to *like* the Grand Canyon. Besides, she wouldn't make the same mistakes. She'd love Europe. She could just feel it. Paris in the summer? Really, what could possibly be better? She couldn't wait to get there and let the adventure of a lifetime begin.

CHAPTER EIGHT

Diana woke to the feeling of someone jostling her arm. Her eyes blinked open, and she was almost surprised to find herself on a Boeing 737 instead of in her bedroom.

"We're here," the woman next to her said, stretching her arms over her head and retying her flowery scarf around her neck. "Thank goodness."

Excitedly, Diana flipped open the shade on the window and looked out upon a dreary tarmac, covered with puddles. The plane was slowly taxiing to the gate. A driving rain spattered against the pane. The buildings in the surrounding area looked much like the ones dotted around JFK. It was dreary and wet, and she had to admit . . . kind of sad.

Well, what am I expecting? It's an airport. Things will be nicer when I get into the city.

The bell overhead dinged, and she grabbed her carry-on and headed for the door. Walking in unison with the other travelers on a mad-dash through the airport, she finally found the baggage claim. Moments later, the baggage began to arrive. The woman she'd traveled next to lifted her own case and said, "Good luck!" almost like a challenge.

Diana smiled and waved. "Same to you," she said, thinking, *I don't need good luck. If I were home right now, I'd be eating Lean Cuisine for One and thinking about how quiet the house is. This is so much better!*

As she reached forward to grab her own suitcase from the carousel, a man jumped in front of her. At first, she thought he was going to help her. But then he yanked a giant duffle bag, nearly smacking Diana in the chest with it. She staggered backward, but not before he stepped on her foot as he turned around.

"*Recules, hors de mon chemin!*" the scruffy man shouted as he whirled. Seven years of French, and she had no clue what that meant. She was about to excuse herself when he said, "*Idiote.*"

She gasped in shock. Yes, it'd been a long time since she'd taken French, but . . . did he just call her an idiot?

"*Excusez-moi*," she snapped with attitude since now she had to scurry around the carousel and chase after her bag. When she finally hefted it up, plenty of people were standing around, but no one offered to help as she struggled to right it on solid ground.

She extended the retractable handle and wheeled it out to the curb where a scowling taxi driver was smoking a cigarette and watching her like he wanted to kill her. He seemed annoyed when she stopped in front of him, and gave her a *What do you want?* glare. Before she could break out her Basic French, he flicked his cigarette butt into the wet street, grabbed her bag, and threw it in the trunk without so much as a "*Bonjour.*"

Was it just her, or was everyone in a bad mood? The rain poured on the roof as she got inside the cabin and pulled out her itinerary. "*Le Bonne Auberge,*" she said, studying her information. "On *Rue de Charonne,* please."

The man grunted and swerved out into the traffic so fast that Diana jerked forward in her seat. She settled herself back and tried to spy interesting Parisian landmarks, but instead, they went about half a mile before they were packed on a five-lane road in wall-to-wall traffic. The driver was heavy on his brakes, so the car kept lurching forward and stopping, lurching and stopping, until Diana's neck hurt from the whiplash. *Huh. This reminds me of something. Oh, right. My commute to work.*

She sighed at her itinerary and then looked at the clock. Well, they'd arrived on time. Early, actually. And she'd gotten her luggage. She put two big check-marks next to the first items on her itinerary, feeling a small bit of satisfaction. But now, those forty-five minutes she'd allowed for getting to the hotel seemed like a bit of an underestimation.

Great. She pulled out her pen and scribbled out the time for *Arrival at hotel,* pushing things back another fifteen minutes. That was okay. She'd just spend forty-five minutes enjoying her pastry at the café, instead of an hour. Not a big deal.

Unfortunately, the taxi driver seemed to be lost. She didn't know this at first; but she got the picture when he pulled off the highway, cruised over to the side of the road, and got out, leaving her alone in the car. He walked to the sidewalk and started conversing loudly with what looked like a homeless man on the corner, since he was buried under a Hefty bag to get out of the rain. They were pointing in all different directions like traffic cops. Then the homeless guy got a cigarette for his efforts, which the driver lit for him. Finally, the driver got back into the car and muttered something in French. Probably a curse word.

"Is everything all right?" she asked him, leaning forward. She leaned back when she realized he smelled as much of body odor as he did of cigarette smoke.

He didn't answer. She wasn't sure if he could speak English.

She shrunk into the seat, a bit annoyed, when something caught her eye in the distance. "Oh! That's the Eiffel Tower!" she cried, nearly pressing her nose up against the window. She fumbled for her phone and took a terrible picture of only the left side of the structure, another car's hood in the way.

He drove a little more, and this time, she looked out the window, camera at the ready, expecting to get a better look. Unfortunately, the next time she saw it . . . it was *farther* away.

She leaned in between the seats. "Are we sure we're going the right—" she stopped when something rose up on the right side of her. "That's the Seine, isn't it? And oh! It's Notre Dame!"

More terrible pictures. This time, she was close enough to get most of it, but she also got the reflection of the window's glass and all the raindrops too. She tried powering down the window, but it appeared to be stuck. As they rode along, she frowned as they passed an overflowing garbage can. In fact, there was a lot of trash in the street. Homeless people meandered along the street. One of them appeared to be peeing in the gutter. It was nothing like the photographs she'd gazed on online.

When they drove down another street, she saw the small café she'd planned to eat at. Her itinerary was on her lap, practically screaming at her. In it, she was supposed to be eating there in fifteen minutes, anyway. Her marketing director side took over. "You know what?" she said to him quickly. "Pull over here. I'll be fine. Thanks."

He seemed all too glad to be rid of her. He cruised to the curb and let her off, disappearing almost the second she swiped her credit card and stepped out to find her bag . . . waiting for her on the curb in a puddle.

She wheeled it toward the café with its striped awning dripping all over the fenced-in eating area. All the umbrellas were closed and the metal tables, wet. It looked depressing.

She went inside the café to find it packed and smelling more of body odor than of delicious coffee and baked goods. There wasn't a seat to be found. Lugging her bag inside, she lifted it up into her arms when she realized it was causing a bottleneck at the door. She stood there for a few moments, waiting. Every time she saw an opening at a table, someone else swooped in and took it. Finally, a man with a goatee stood up from a high table in the corner. She pounced on it, throwing her elbows on it to claim it before she realized it was covered with powdered sugar and something sticky. Grimacing, she wiped at the fabric of her shirt, noticing an odd brown stain there. Caramel, maybe. *Lovely.*

A waitress with a messy bun and one eyebrow raised in a rather disinterested way sauntered over to her, pad at the ready. *"Oui?"*

Staring at her itinerary, she decided now was as good a time as any to try out her rusty French and order that *mille fieule* she'd seen on the website for the place. It had looked delicious. She said, in the best accent she could muster, channeling Stéphane, *"Puis-je prendre un café et un mille fieule, s'il vous plait."* Can I please have a coffee and a *mille fieule?*

The woman stared at her like she had something wedged between her front teeth. Then she said simply, "No."

Diana looked around. At the many packed tables surrounding her, people were enjoying coffees and pastries. Why couldn't she? Was this because she was American? She'd heard the long-standing rumor about how the French didn't particularly care for Americans, which was actually why she'd been reluctant to talk to Stéphane at first. But he'd proven her wrong, *definitely,* and since then all she had to do was hear someone speaking in a French accent to have a warm, fuzzy feeling inside.

This had to just be a misunderstanding. "Um . . . *café?"*

The waitress nodded, a brooding look on her face. *"Oui . . .et . . .?"*

Okay, at least she was getting somewhere now. But she'd really wanted that French pastry. The woman stared at her, impatient, so Diana blurted the first thing that came to her mind. "Croissant?"

The woman nodded and rushed away into the swell of the crowd.

48

Okay, no *mille fieule*. If that was the worst thing that happened, it was no tragedy.

Diana let out the breath she'd been holding and looked around. The place was hot and stuffy and cramped with a low ceiling that seemed in danger of crushing them, and now—a new odor greeted her nostrils. Someone—or many someones—had recently smoked cigarettes because, though there was no smoke in the air, the stench was thicker than it had been in the cab. That and . . . something that strongly smelled like urine.

Trying to breathe through her mouth, she rummaged through her purse and pulled out her hand sanitizer. Giving herself a little spritz, she found her phone. As she did, she noticed two men, probably the age of Bea, staring intently at her. They wore t-shirts and faded jeans, and they were unshaven. Their hair was long and unkempt. One of them had a man-bun, and the other had a Rastafarian beanie.

Before she could look away, one of the men smiled a surly smile, licked his lips, and winked.

Oh, no, he did not do that, she thought, her face flaming. She was no cougar; she had no intention of following in Evan's footsteps. Not ever. Evan may have been a surgeon, but deep down, he was very simple. Probably because his work became so stressful, he preferred people as easy and uncomplicated as he could get them. Thus, Tilda. But *those* men, the ones leering at her? She *knew* what they were after, and it wasn't her age-old wisdom and thought-provoking conversation.

She grabbed her itinerary and stared at it, her cheeks still stinging red. She was about to blow it out of the water, big time. And right then, she didn't really care. So far, nothing about Paris had been very good. Why had she thought it was so wonderful?

One word came to mind at that moment: *Stéphane.*

If he had been here, everything about this place would be different . . . she knew it. She'd be here—and in love, and isn't that what they said? *There is no place like Paris when you're in love.*

When you're alone, maybe it just . . . sucked.

Calm yourself, Diana. You have only been in France for an hour. It is bound to get better. Just think of Versailles. It's going to be amazing.

Yes, it would be. But it still would be better with company.

Before she could stop herself, she lifted her phone and quickly tapped in *Stéphane de Fonblanque.*

The Google results were as they'd been before. Limited. There was only one mention of the *de Fonblanque* family, an entry stating that they'd owned property in Nantes in the late 1800's, and a flat in Paris, in *Saint-Germain-des-Prés*. But that was all.

It made sense. He'd told her that, as a member of nobility, his family had a duty to stay largely out of the public eye and not cause too much scandal. At least his father had been extremely strict with Stéphane, telling him that he needed to keep a low profile in America, which was why he'd been so secretive about it around her.

She stared at the address as the waitress came by with her coffee and croissant. As she set it down, Diana said, *"Excusez-moi,"* and pointed to the address on her phone. *"Où est-ce?"*

The girl finally lost the disinterested look. Now, she raised both eyebrows, clearly impressed. Obviously, it must've been a nice neighborhood. Then she started to spout off directions that made Diana's head spin.

"Hold on," Diana said sheepishly. "Could you say that slower?"

"Arrondissement six," she said.

"Arrond—what? I'm sorry. I don't understand."

As she tried to remember how to translate that into French, the woman said, "Oh, you're American," as if that explained some things. She pointed outside and said, "The arrondissement. They are our neighborhoods. Six is that way. You'll have to go past the cathedral. Cross the river. Just keep walking, and you'll see the signs. It's about a twenty-minute walk. You really can't miss Arrondisement six. Just look for the people with their noses so high in the air that airplanes need to watch out for them." She chuckled at her own joke.

"Thank you," Diana said. The waitress left, and she tore off a piece of the croissant and popped it in her mouth. It was still warm, flaky, buttery, and absolutely delicious.

So maybe things were looking up.

As she stared at the address, she couldn't help wondering . . . was Stéphane there? Would he be at the ball? Would he remember her?

No, as much as she'd tried to tell herself she hadn't come here for him, part of her couldn't help wondering, wanting to make good on that promise she'd made to him all those years ago. And perhaps he was at that house, alone, and thinking of her too. If they were indeed meant for each other, then it was only natural.

50

And I'm here for adventure, she thought, gobbling down the last of the croissant. *So it's about time I had one. Right now.*

*

Oh, I've totally blown my itinerary out of the water.

That's what Diana thought as she walked down *Rue Madame,* balancing her trusty travel umbrella in one hand and rolling her bag on the cracked sidewalk behind her with the other. Every so often, it'd get caught in a rut, and she'd have to pull it free.

After she traversed the Seine, over a rather large bridge that didn't look anything like the quaint ones she'd seen in photographs, she came across the Paris she'd dreamed of. Little outdoor cafes with tables behind dainty wrought-iron fences. Tiny shops—like a little housewares shop that sold the most adorable gingham-check kitchen ensemble and a bookstore full of old volumes called Shakespeare and Company.

She passed several well-dressed well-to-do people on the street, but nobody even looked at her, much less greeted her. Not very much different from New York, and yet for some reason, she'd expected more.

This section of town was clearly swanky with fences around the trees lining the streets and stately homes with marble facades, all lined together, shoulder to shoulder. There were iron benches and streetlamps at healthy intervals, and, every once in a while, the line of buildings would break to allow for an ivy-covered gate, a narrow passage along a crumbling cobbled path to a wildly romantic hidden courtyard, perhaps.

She stopped when she reached the address on Google, and stared up at the door, which had at oval-shaped window on the center. It stood behind an imposing iron gate.

But that was the only thing regal about it.

Because most of it was, simply . . . gone.

She checked the address again, then once more. This couldn't be right.

The whole building had been ripped down, almost to the studs. It was just a rusting skeleton standing upon a pile of white rubble. It had been completely gutted. There was a sign in one of the holes that had once been a window that said *Blanchette Construction.*

51

Whoever had once lived there, decades ago, clearly wasn't living there now.

Well, it had been *nearly* thirty years ago. He could be anywhere now. In fact, maybe he wasn't even alive anymore.

Diana looked up and down the street, and for the briefest moment, she felt like she might cry. It was silly. She hadn't come here for Stéphane.

Or had she?

Wasn't that the reason she was standing here right now, instead of browsing the Louvre or riding to the top of the Eiffel Tower? If she'd only come here to take in the sights of Paris, she wouldn't have looked him up. She wouldn't have put all those places he spoke of on her itinerary. And she very likely wouldn't have bought a ticket to that ball.

Really, what was the reason she was here—now? Was it for the thrill of traveling and seeing new sights . . . or was it for something else? Some crazy pipe dream that really was as ridiculous as Lily and Bea had made it out to be?

And maybe that pipe dream had disappeared a long time ago when she decided to decline that invitation. Some doors opened for a short time and could never be reopened. Maybe she was only fooling herself, even entertaining the idea.

At that moment, her phone buzzed with a text. She looked at it. A message from Lily: *Did your plane land? Are you all right?*

She texted that she was fine, but she wasn't sure.

Was she all right? Here she was in a place she'd dreamed of for years, and yet, though the surroundings were what she'd wanted, everything else felt wrong. Maybe this was a mistake. That's what they'd all said back home, hadn't they? *You're making a mistake.* Maybe she should've listened, instead of quitting her job and rushing head-first into this.

She fisted her hand around her suitcase handle and continued on, batting those thoughts away from her mind.

If it *was* a mistake, the worst thing she could do was wallow in it. No, she was going to own it. Make the most of it. She was going to go to that ball tomorrow and try to have a good time, no matter what. Stéphane or not.

CHAPTER NINE

Thank goodness things began looking up. The rain slowed to a mere drizzle, and the driver of the second cab Diana hailed knew where to find the inn.

The place was across from a park full of blooming dogwood trees, their white petals raining down over the street as she stepped onto the curb. The building itself was a brownstone with three stories of balconies with iron railings of intricate scrollwork. It was set back from the road a bit to allow for a small circular drive with a fountain in the very center, dribbling over a goddess, arms outstretched as if she was holding up the sky. A small sign outside the door said, *Le Bonne Auberge.* The valet took her small bag and opened the door for her.

Inside, the place was modest but well-appointed. It wasn't one of those spectacular hotels with the massive multi-story foyer, like were popular among the chain hotels. She'd selected something quaint and boutique, hoping it'd give her the flavor of Europe, and this definitely succeeded. There was a small nook on either side, full of comfortable leather couches and mismatched-fabric Queen Anne-style chairs, one situated around a fireplace, the other around a small piano.

There was a small station with fresh-baked pastries and lemon water near the check-in desk in the rear of the room. She stared at the croissants and the assortment of jams, mouthwatering. *If I'd just come here first, I could've killed two agenda birds with one stone,* she thought, checking her phone. It was after three. If she checked in right away, she might be able to head over to the Eiffel Tower and salvage some of her to-do list for the day.

Her growling stomach protested that.

She clamped a hand over it and approached the check-in. "Hello."

"*Bonjour,*" the Asian woman behind the desk said pleasantly with a French accent. Despite looking about the age of one of Diana's daughters, she was wearing a sophisticated pale pink cashmere sweater that Diana would've worn. "Checking in?"

"That's right. I'm Diana St. James. I have a reservation."

"Good to have you staying with us, Ms. St. James," the woman said, tapping something into her computer. "Is this your first time in Paris?"

She nodded.

"Well, welcome. We have you in one of our penthouse suites for three days, correct?"

"Yes," she said, her stomach growling even louder now as she handed over her American Express.

The clerk must've heard it, because she smiled as she continued to type. "Please help yourself to one of our complimentary pastries."

Diana laughed, "I think I need something more substantial."

The lady smiled, not looking up from her computer. "You may have more than one."

I could eat the whole tray, Diana thought and was not exaggerating in the least. "Well . . ."

The clerk passed over a folio which contained the keycard and said, "If you'd like to go to your room, the elevator is behind you. Otherwise, the inn's restaurant is through those doors. They're serving lunch now."

Diana followed her pointing finger to a set of double doors behind the piano. "Perfect," she said, gathering her things and navigating around the furniture. As she walked, she noticed a French newspaper on the coffee table. As she paused to try to translate the headline, the elevator doors dinged open and a voice called, "Ah, Annie, what's the story?" with an Irish accent.

The woman behind the desk giggled. "Fine, Sean, and you?"

Diana looked over her shoulder to see a man with a beard checking out the rack with brochures from different attractions. As he did, he took a cup and tipped the lever on the decanter one-handed, pouring himself a cup of water, which he swallowed in a single gulp.

"Have a great day, Annie!" he said as Diana turned away and headed toward the restaurant. She found herself in a small cozy pub, all dark cherry wood with a small bar on the end and only a couple of tables. Coats of arms, French flags, and war memorabilia decorated the walls. Because it was three in the afternoon, the place was empty.

Diana hovered there, wondering if it was indeed open because there didn't even seem to be a hostess.

"You can just seat yourself, dear," the man, Sean's, voice called behind her. He strolled in and took a seat at the bar. "Fancy a pint?"

She walked in, a little dazed, and slipped onto the barstool next to him. She hadn't liked beer before she came here, and she'd never envisioned wasting her few chances to explore the French culinary scene by having one now. "I'm actually starving," she said. "I came here for lunch."

"Well, let me tell you, lass. I'm thirsty," he winked.

Magically, a man appeared behind the bar. Sean looked at her and said, "The lady was here first."

"Oh—" She grabbed a menu. "You can go. I'm not sure what I want yet."

Sean grinned at the man and lifted a finger. Somehow, that was signal enough for the bartender to pour him a draft of thick stout with a heavy brown foam. Something told Diana that this was not his first stop in this establishment.

"You're Irish?" she asked him, looking up from her menu. The bartender was standing there, so she just said, "Coffee. Black."

"Aye. You're . . . American," he said, seeming pleased with himself for making the connection. He rubbed his gray beard. "I'm thinking New York?"

"Impressive. How did you know?"

"I'm good with dialects," he said, smiling. "I know *cawfee* when I hear it."

She laughed as the bartender poured her the coffee, then leaned forward, and took a sip. When she looked up, he was extending his hand.

"Sean. What's your name, lass?"

She shook it. "Diana. Are you here on vacation?"

"You could say that. I'm just tottering about. Had a bit of business to tend to but that's over, so now I'm just taking it easy. Thinking I might extend it a little, go all over this fair land of ours," He took a big gulp of his beer. "You?"

"Oh, this is my first day in Paris. Hopefully the first of many days in Europe. I'm planning to stay the year if all goes well."

"Is that right? Well, good on you. How're you liking it so far?"

"It's a little different from what I imagined," she admitted, "But I haven't really done anything on my itinerary yet."

She patted the notebook, which she'd laid on the bar by her purse.

"Itinerary? Let me have a look."

She slid it over to him, sure he'd rib her when he saw just how uptight she was when it came to planning. Judging from his relaxed manner and wrinkled shirt, he seemed more like a fly-by-the-seat-of-his-pants guy. But he simply looked it over, nodding.

"How much have you seen so far?"

The bartender stopped by. She looked over the menu, ordered the *salade Parisianne,* since it sounded quintessentially French, and shrugged at her new friend, "Nothing, actually. I got a little lost in the cab, and I just checked in. Not to mention, the rain . . ."

"Right. It was bucketing down, before. But you've got all the good ones in here," he said, turning the page. "You're going to Versailles tomorrow, eh? That's a nice place." He whistled.

"Oh, yes. You've been?"

"Oh yes. Got lost there, plenty of times."

She laughed, "I'm going for a special event. It's a masquerade ball, right on the grounds. People dress in period costumes, and it goes all night long with dancing and fireworks and food. Have you heard of it?"

He shook his head, "Can't say that I have. But that place is as big as all of Ballygangargin."

Her brow rose in confusion, "Bally . . ."

"Ballygangargin. My town. Smack in the middle of Ireland. Ever hear of it?" He chuckled to himself, "Of course you haven't. No one ever has. I own the Ballygangargin Pub. You should hear people try to pronounce it when they're wankered. Not a pretty sight."

She laughed as he drained the rest of his glass and held up a finger for another. The man was possibly too fond of his beer, but there was no doubt he was fun. Stout and built solidly—like a refrigerator, he was nothing like lean, lanky Evan, and yet she didn't mind that. Maybe she didn't mind the kind of guy whose shirts always needed ironing. He was fun, lighthearted, and maybe that was just what she needed.

And now that she really had a chance to look at him, he was handsome with twinkling eyes and an infectious smile. She scanned his hands on the bar and noticed no wedding ring. "When do you go back to Ireland?" she asked him.

"Not in any rush. Don't have anyone home, waiting for me. So that's why I'm giving serious consideration to tottering." He looked her over. "That's why you surprise me, lass. You traveling alone?"

She nodded.

"No man would let a lovely woman like yourself travel alone," he said with a smile as he swept his beer off the bar. "What are you running away from?"

Her face heated. It'd been a long time since any man had called her lovely. "I'm not running away. I'm just . . ." She paused. She really hadn't expected to get into this with anyone. But he was asking, and for some reason, she felt like he'd understand. "I'm in the midst of a divorce, and I realized it'd been a long time since I did anything for myself. I've always wanted to go to that ball—since I was in college. So I quit my job, bought a ticket to the ball, and here I am. I know it sounds crazy, but . . ."

"Not at all. It makes right good sense if you're asking me."

"You think so?" When he nodded emphatically, she smiled, feeling very comfortable around him. She hadn't even felt this relaxed around Evan, even though he'd been her back-up to Stéphane. It was only after a few drinks that she felt at ease with him . . . really, with any man. She wagered Sean would be a lot of fun out on a date.

In fact, it'd make her grand entrance at the ball so much nicer to have someone to walk in with. Not only that, he'd seemed fun-loving . . . as if he'd embrace the whole period-style costume thing. Maybe . . .

"So you don't have any plans for the rest of your trip?" she asked him, fishing.

"Not a one," he said, peering at his beer. "Though I'd wager whatever I do, it'll involve a few more of these."

Her salad came, and unfortunately, it looked about as appetizing as Paris itself had when she'd first arrived—with wilting lettuce, croutons, and not much else other than a drippy looking sunny-side up egg. But now her stomach wasn't rumbling for food. It was from nerves.

As the bartender went away, leaving them alone, she poked at it with her fork, trying to work up the courage to ask him. Could she? With Stéphane, with Evan, they'd always asked *her*. She'd never actually had to. But why not? Why couldn't she?

"Would you go back to Versailles?"

He stared at her, his eyes narrowed in confusion, and paused a beat too long.

"What I mean is . . . would you be interested in . . ." She placed her fork down. "Would you ever go to a ball like that? Like I'm going to? I mean, sometimes I think it's silly—me, a grown woman, wanting to go to the ball alone, where you dress up in ridiculous costumes and . . ."

"No. Sounds like a craic, if you ask me," he answered, tone earnest.

"A . . . what?"

"A good time. You know, whatever floats your boat."

"Oh." She took a deep breath. "Would you . . ."

She drew it out so long that she began to feel her courage leaving her by the second. Then she looked over the bar and saw the bartender, gazing at her, an indecipherable smirk on his face as if he was watching a particularly good episode of his favorite sitcom.

She cleared her throat as her eyes drifted to the bar—"Pass me the pepper, please?"

He turned to the bar and swept the crystal jar of pepper over to her. She shook it vigorously over her salad, not really knowing if it needed it or not.

It would be better to go alone. After all, she was fifty-two years old, not twenty-two. She wasn't Evan, who could slip back into that world of new relationships so easily. She simply couldn't date. She wasn't even sure she really wanted to. Dating involved expectations and primping oneself to look good and analyzing words and wondering will-we-or-will-we not . . . it was exhausting. And she'd come to have fun, not exhaust herself.

Sean polished off his second pint and set the glass down on the bar with too much force. He reached into his wallet, threw a few euros down, and stood up. "Wonderful meeting you, lass. Enjoy your trip. Perhaps I'll see you again sometime," he said with a smile, striding away before she could even say goodbye.

She had to wonder if that was a *Sliding Doors* moment, too, like the one with Stéphane, and if she would come to regret not being bold and asking for what she wanted. For a moment, she hoped she wouldn't think of *that* one for the next thirty years too.

But no, that was the old Diana, overthinking every little thing she'd done or was about to do in life. The new Diana was taking life by the horns and enjoying every moment of it—no regrets.

Right then, she made a decision: no more hesitation. While sightseeing and especially at the ball tomorrow, she'd own her life, make bold choices, take risks, and never back down.

CHAPTER TEN

The following day, Diana went sightseeing. She only had the morning and early afternoon to explore, since she wanted to be back by three to get ready for the ball, so she decided to explore the area of the Eleventh Arrondissement by foot. From her map, she discovered that the Bastille wasn't far away, so she hoped she could get in a few pictures of the plaza on her way to *Saint Chapelle,* since Stéphane had said it was the most beautiful church in Paris, and, of course, Notre Dame, which wasn't far away.

Unfortunately, even with her map firmly in hand, she wound up getting turned around and ended up at *Père Lachaise* Cemetery. *A rather morbid start to your year in Europe, isn't this, Diana?* she thought with a smile. *I hope this isn't a portent of things to come.*

As she went inside, she googled the website and learned the locations of all the famous people buried there: Jim Morrison, Marie Callas, Oscar Wilde, Balzac, Chopin. She walked down the cobbled path, the shade of the oak trees shielding her from the bright hot sun, and stood in front of Chopin's grave, with the statue of a beautiful angel seated above it, head bent in despair, holding her silent harp. People had left offerings of flowers, in various stages of decay, and coins and trinkets to the great composer. Someone had left a tiny toy piano.

"Maybe you can tell me, Frédéric," she whispered, looking around to make sure no one else was nearby, "Why it is that I keep striking out when trying to find the things I'm looking for in this city? I keep finding ghosts. Figments of things that may or may not be there."

Silence.

Not that she expected more.

"Well," she said, "Maybe Jim Morrison will have more to say."

She walked along farther, marveling over the many statues and remembrances—some beautiful and sad, some grotesque, some downright horrifying. She stopped at the square headstone of one Joseph Fournier, an 18th century mathematician, according to the display on her phone. A white-faced ghoulish creature with no discernable nose peered back at her with wild wide eyes.

"That is truly terrifying," she said aloud, as she continued on.

Maybe this *was* a portent of things to come. No, not that she'd end up in the ground at the end of the year—she truly hoped not, though Lily seemed to think it was a definite possibility with all the axe-murderers around. But would she always be meandering about, getting side-tracked and led off itinerary, never being able to see the things she truly wanted to see or do what she wanted to do?

If so, it was a perfect metaphor for her life thus far.

Sure, she'd done a lot. There wasn't a thing about her past she wasn't proud of. She'd had wonderful children, a good career. Even her marriage had been good—for a time. But they were all happy accidents. None of those things had been the result of doing exactly what she wanted.

"If it kills me, I'm going to see the sights I *want*," she said in a loud voice, so loud that a couple of other tourists looked at her like she was insane.

She shrugged and continued on, feeling lighter and more resolved. As she did, she made a mental list: *Rent the most gorgeous costume at Versailles, no matter what the expense. Be outgoing and talk with as many people as possible. Dance with at least one handsome man. Be the envy of the ballroom floor. Make this night absolutely unforgettable . . .*

Some of the things got jumbled in her head, but the last one hung there. *Make this night absolutely unforgettable . . .*

Yes. Tonight, at Versailles, she would do everything she wanted. Every last thing.

*

But by the time she left the cemetery and got herself a chicken taco—yes, she realized she was in France but aromas coming from the food truck were positively stop-in-her-tracks deadly—it was almost one. There was absolutely no way she could retrace her steps, go all the way to *Saint Chapelle* and Notre Dame, and be back at a reasonable hour.

Maybe there's something else in my itinerary that's nearby, she said, licking the taco grease off her fingers and reaching into her bag for the notebook. *I should also write down my itinerary for tonight. Make this night absolutely unforgettable . . .*

After rummaging for a few moments, she gasped.

It was big. Full. Took up most of the space in her purse. And now, she realized . . . it was gone.

"I must've left it in the hotel," she said aloud, remembering how she'd been studying it the prior night before bed, trying to salvage her sightseeing time. She could even picture it, sitting right on the night table. "I can't believe I forgot it."

She rushed back to the hotel, and with every step she felt more naked. She'd never gone into a board meeting without her trusty folio with her agenda. It might as well have been surgically attached to her hip; it was that dear to her.

But she'd been out of sorts that morning after getting another text from Lily. Even though she'd responded that everything was great, Lily had said, *You just don't sound happy.* Diana had laughed. All she'd written were two words: *Everything's great!!* As if Lily could sense her unease all the way across the Atlantic?

When Diana had responded, asking what she meant, Lily had said: *You never use double punctuation in your texts.*

That was very true. It seemed like overkill. She'd responded, *Don't be silly, I am doing wonderfully. Off to see the Bastille plaza and Notre Dame!*

That time, she'd been careful with her punctuation.

But it was very possible she could've just been so busy responding to Lily's texts that she'd forgotten to stick the notebook in her bag.

When she got back to the inn, she quickly took the elevator up to the third floor, exploded into the room, and stared at the night table.

There was nothing there.

A creeping sensation tickled its way up the back of Diana's neck as she surveyed the room. Housekeeping had been there, making the bed and setting right the flowered duvet. The towels had been replaced, and the shaggy gray carpet had fresh track marks in it from the vacuum.

Her inn room was very small, but just what she needed. It had a sliver of a view of the Eiffel Tower, too, as promised. But there weren't many hiding spots where the agenda could've gone to. The housekeeper hadn't moved it anywhere in view. All the surfaces in the room were empty.

Helplessly, she started to open drawers. A panicky feeling bloomed in her gut, spiraling out to her chest, crushing her.

If I can't find my agenda, my trip is ruined. I might as well go home!

She stormed around the room in a whirlwind, pulling drawers open and slamming them closed. With every one she opened, she only got more frantic.

"What did I do with it?" she mumbled. It had to be here. Or did it? Maybe she had brought it with her this morning, and it'd fallen out of her bag when she'd gone to grab her map.

Her palms sweated. She could just imagine heading back home and telling everyone she had to turn back because of her agenda. They'd think it silly. But they didn't understand. That agenda was her life. It had so much in there, so much more than just where she was planning to go on a particular day.

"No," she cried, almost near tears. "No, no, no!"

She dove for the small night table drawer, by this time expecting all she'd find was the room service menu since she'd seen it there before.

But atop it, easily visible, was a hint of green. Her agenda. The housekeeper must've tucked it away here.

She grabbed it in her hands and held it against her chest, sighing with relief and intent on never letting it go again. Then she opened it up. Sure enough, everything was there, just as she remembered.

She wiped at her forehead, surprised to find out it was covered in sweat. Then she looked across the room at the mirror. For a second, she didn't recognize herself. That wasn't the Diana St. James who ruled the boardroom at Addict Cosmetics. No, this woman looked wild, manic, like someone who wasn't in control of her life. Someone crazy.

She quickly started to write down the itinerary for tonight, but only two of the things stayed in her mind: *Rent the most gorgeous costume at Versailles, no matter what the expense* and *Make this night absolutely unforgettable . . .*

Tapping the pen against her chin, she tried to remember the rest. Something about dancing. She'd have to think about it later.

Diana set the agenda down and went closer to the mirror. She'd been so proud of the way she aged—her kids said she didn't look a day over thirty-nine—but now, the shadows on her face made her look older. Not to mention, the fear in her eyes brought out wrinkles she never knew she had.

Funny how, no matter how carefully she placed entries into that agenda of hers, things never seemed to turn out the way she wanted. Maybe that kind of control was impossible, and a waste of her time.

She ran her hands over her face, smoothing the wrinkles back, then looked at the time on the clock.

It was nearly time to get ready for the ball.

But as she looked at herself, she made a promise. She'd drink, laugh, dance, and enjoy. This time, she'd be more relaxed. This time, she'd leave the agenda in the drawer, relinquish control, and embrace whatever was going to happen . . . good or bad.

CHAPTER ELEVEN

When Diana stepped off the shuttle to Versailles, she gasped.

Yes, like everyone, she'd seen pictures of the palace. *Many* pictures, especially once Stéphane came into her life. In fact, that had been her favorite pastime in those weeks after he went back to France—staring at photos of the opulent rooms and imagining walking arm in arm with her love. But nothing had quite prepared her for the sheer enormity of the place when she was standing in front of it.

The shuttle dropped her off—still a long walk from the actual building. She and the other people on the bus meandered about the lush gardens which seemed to stretch on forever, gradually coming closer to the main building. Once she climbed the front steps to the massive entrance, a number of employees in period costumes, right down to the powdered wigs, checked her ticket and motioned for her to go into a tent that had been set up on the grounds.

When she went inside, her jaw dropped. The place was full of everything she could possibly need—wigs, jewelry, shoes, and, of course, gowns of every color and fabric. The tent was also full of partygoers, all in the midst of preparing for the big event. Despite a number of fans going at full blast, the air inside was warm and positively buzzing with the excitement. Everyone seemed in a jovial mood.

"Hello, my name is Colette, and I will be helping transform you tonight!" a woman in an ornate Marie Antoinette-style wig and pink gown said, running an eye over Diana from head to toe. "I hope you are ready!"

Getting into the festive spirit of the event and reminding herself to relax, Diana nodded, *"Oui!"*

"You have beautiful pale skin. So lovely. I see something in a ruby red with a low decolletage, yes?"

"Well . . . let's not go too daring," she began. She never wore red—she was used to the New York City uniform, nothing but black, white, and shades between. And a low neckline? She was used to buttoning her blouses all the way up to the top.

A little voice suddenly stopped her. *Remember, relax.*

Diana smiled as Colette led her down the aisle of dresses. "Actually. Whatever you think looks best. I'm placing myself in your capable hands!"

"Lovely!" Colette said, clapping her hands together. "Do you have a budget?"

Diana remembered her first agenda item: *rent the most gorgeous costume at Versailles, no matter what the expense.* "No. Not at all. You have my permission not to look at price tags."

"Wonderful! That makes it so fun!" She studied Diana's body carefully. "You're a size ten, US, yes?"

Diana's mouth opened slightly, "Y-yes. Wow. You're very good."

From that point on, Diana had no reservations or doubts in Colette's abilities. Colette picked out a lovely shimmering burgundy-red gown with cream-colored lace accents. It fit Diana perfectly after Colette helped tie her into the corset and undergarments. When she stepped in front of the mirror, Diana was astounded. She looked beautiful, almost like she belonged to the time period.

"Oh, this is nice," she said, wiggling to get her ribs used to the corset. If it weren't for that, she might have even wished she lived in the time period. She pulled on the lace-edged neck of the dress, which was definitely low-cut, feeling rather bare until she reminded herself that she'd made a promise to go with the flow. Besides, she was so used to covering up that what was daring to her was actually tame compared to some of the things her daughters wore.

When Diana came out of the dressing room and gave her the thumbs-up, Colette presented her with a pair of matching heels. "Size nine, right?"

"Yes. That's right." She stepped into them, expecting them to be uncomfortable. Instead, they fit like her slippers back at home. She lifted the layers of fabric and swished them at her hips as she moved in front of the mirror once more, admiring herself. "It's beautiful."

"It'll be even nicer once I finish your hair and makeup," Colette said, sitting her down in a barber's chair. "Would you like a wig? You have such lovely hair. It'd be a shame to cover it."

"I think not," she said, looking at the choices. They were like works of art themselves, but it was hot outside, and she could just imagine her scalp sweating and itching like crazy. "Can you do something with my hair?"

Colette raked her fingers though Diana's dark curls and smiled, "Can I? Your hair is so thick and beautiful. Just wait and see what I do!"

To keep Diana in suspense, Colette turned her chair away from the mirror and took out her curling iron. Diana had masses of thick hair, so Colette chatted away about the party as she got to work taming it. "I usually work in the palace, giving tours most of the time. But this is my favorite night of the year. I love doing makeovers for our guests. This is my fifth year doing the ball."

"You've been to five of these? What is it like?"

"Oh, well, of course I have to stay here helping guests most of the time, but they let us go out on shifts to enjoy, and it's amazing," she gushed. "Absolutely beautiful. Almost magical, really. It's like for one night every year, this place is transported back in time to its pre-revolution splendor and excess. And it's like you can almost see Marie Antoinette and Louis XVI and their court, walking the halls. The ball itself takes place in the luxurious Hall of Mirrors—that's the most famous ballroom in the world."

"The one with all the gold—right?—and those huge crystal chandeliers? I've seen it in pictures!"

She rolled a curl in the front of Diana's face. "That's right. It's beautiful, no? You'll also be able to tour some of the other rooms. Not all of them, of course. I've been here five years and even I have not seen all of them. There are 2,300, all told."

Diana gasped.

"Of course you'll be able to walk the gardens, and there will be entertainment everywhere. Drinks and buffet throughout the night. And of course, fireworks!" she laughed. "It's really so much fun. I do hope you enjoy."

"I'm sure I will," she said, her heart fluttering under the cape that Colette had laid over her chest to protect the dress.

Colette carefully painted Diana's eyelids and applied what looked like a bright red lipstick to her lips. Yet another thing Diana wasn't used to—she usually wore colorless lip gloss and little makeup—but she repeated her mantra—*Let it go, just enjoy*—over and over in her head as Colette finished and dabbed her face with a big powder puff.

"I think we are in business!" Colette said with a smile, removing the cape with great flourish. She took Diana's hand and led her to a full-length mirror. "Ladies and Gentlemen of the court, may I present the distinguished Mademoiselle Diana St. James, from New York City, the United States of America!"

Diana blinked at herself in the mirror. Just as the last time she'd glimpsed herself in the mirror in the hotel, she hardly recognized herself. This time, though, it was in a good way. Her hair was piled up upon her head in ringlets, and several curls draped loose over her bare collarbones and neck. The makeup was definitely dramatic—the dark colors making her brown eyes pop, and her lips looked fuller. Her skin shimmered slightly with the light powder. Collette had even applied the trademark Marie Antoinette birthmark to her cheek.

"What do you think?" Collette asked hopefully.

"Oh, it's beautiful. You're a miracle worker!" Diana said with a smile.

"Well, it was a pleasure," Colette said, handing her the folio that would include her bill. "Oops! I forgot! You're not done yet. The *piece de resistance*."

She lifted a delicate gold mask and placed it over Diana's eyes.

"Ah. Yes, perfect."

Now, she had the air of mystery. Also . . . bonus, it covered her crow's feet.

Not for the first time, Diana felt a thrill of anticipation shoot up and down her spine.

Colette gave her a little hug. "Now, I must say goodbye. You're going to want to go to the next station, over that way. There, you can rent jewelry to match your ensemble."

"Thank you," Diana said, following Colette's pointed finger down the crowded aisle to the next station. There, she saw several glass jewel cases, full of the gorgeous gems.

At first, she thought they must be costume jewelry, but as she neared them, a man said, "Are you kidding me? Two thousand euros to rent for a few hours? You're out of your mind, Gladys."

His wife, an older woman, pouted, "But they're diamonds, and they don't come cheap. Plus, it goes so perfectly with this dress!"

Real jewels?

Diana leaned in and looked at the jewels. Yes, they were beautiful, but Diana had never been impressed by such things. She'd always kept her jewelry to a minimum. Even the engagement ring Evan gave her was a modest diamond fleck. It simply never interested her.

Right away, she spotted an enormous diamond-and-ruby pendant, the exact color of her dress. *That's how they get you—hook, line, and sinker,* she reminded herself, preparing to turn away. *I'm no dummy. I've never cared for jewelry, and I'm not going to start now. No way am I spending that much to rent a piece of jewelry.*

A male voice called behind the case, "This one—the esteemed Madame Royale—would look lovely on you, *mademoiselle.*"

She turned back to see a young man with the bluest eyes, gazing at her. He was wearing the traditional ascot and waistcoat, and one of those ridiculous wigs—this one, iridescent pink. He had an over-powdered face and dark lipstick that matched the Marie Antoinette mole on his chin. The lipstick was, incidentally, also on his front teeth, a fact she noticed right away when he smiled at her as he opened the case.

"Come, now. Let us just slip it on and see, shall we?"

Diana held up her palm to him and prepared to turn away. "No. It's all right. I'm fine."

He tutted with disappointment, "Ah, but I'm gifted in these things. The jewelry speaks to me. Can you hear it?" He cupped a hand around his ear and pretended to listen intently. "It's saying something, quite insistently."

She shook her head. Who was this character? "Sorry. Jewelry *doesn't—*"

"Maybe you haven't taken the time to listen. And right now, this piece is saying it only wants to be worn by you," he said, reaching into the case for something else. "It comes with gold earrings, too, but I daresay that all a beauty like you needs is the necklace."

What, does this guy think I was born yesterday? She shook her head.

He clutched at his chest, "Oh, you wound me. I feel it's my life's work to find the jewelry to complement these gowns, and I'm afraid my life will not be complete unless you leave here wearing this necklace. It's truly meant for you."

They definitely hired good salesmen for these jobs, ones that didn't know the word "no." But Diana refused to be swayed. She cracked open the folio and looked at the damage so far. She nearly choked as she mentally translated the euros to dollars. Almost four thousand dollars? She grabbed a fan from atop the jewelry case, opened it, and waved it furiously to cool her hot cheeks. *"Really.* No. I can't. It's already been a lot more than what I was hoping to spend."

Even as she said it, the words she'd scrawled in her agenda came back to her: *rent the most gorgeous costume at Versailles, no matter what the expense.* That included jewelry. And really, the ensemble was not complete without a little jewelry.

"Just for fun, darling?" he said, undoing the clasp and pouting as he held it out, ready to be slipped over her neck.

She checked the time. She'd gotten to Versailles so early that it was still another hour before the garden tours began. And the salesman was staring at her with a little pout on his burgundy lips. She rolled her eyes and turned away from him so he could put it on, "Very well."

He carefully settled the gem in place and tightened the clasp around her neck. It was a substantial piece and felt heavy against her chest. "Is it paste?"

"Oh, no. The Madame Royale is absolutely real and one of the most striking necklaces ever created. Twenty-four rubies surrounding one very precious eighteen-carat diamond."

She gasped.

"Oui, it is the most expensive item in our collection here, available for rental," he went on. "It was worn by the beautiful Marie Therese, who eventually donated it back to the estate before her death. Its price for tonight is ten thousand euros, but it's worth millions."

Millions of dollars. Around her neck. She almost giggled, how ridiculous it was. This was so, as Beatrice would say, *extra.* Unnecessary. She'd loved the way she looked before, and that was fine.

She almost told him to take it right off, that it wasn't "speaking" to her, but then she sighed and spun around.

And the second she did, she regretted it.

He angled an oval lighted mirror toward her and grinned, "What did I tell you, *mademoiselle? Fantastique!"*

That was an understatement. There were few times when Diana looked into the mirror and was actually pleased with what she saw these days. Most times, she'd find another errant gray hair she'd have to pluck, or some unpleasant wrinkle that hadn't been there the day before. But she had to admit this ensemble was absolutely breathtaking now. She'd heard people say that jewelry could "pull an outfit together," but she never truly understood the meaning of that, until now. It didn't overwhelm her at all; in fact, it complemented her entire image—almost as if it was part of her.

"Oh," was all she could say.

The salesman took her hand and dropped two teardrop white-and-red-stoned earrings into her palm. "You might as well wear these, too."

He didn't have to coax her this time. She immediately snapped one onto each lobe.

Very nice.

She'd nearly entered into a dream sequence—one where she appeared at the top step of a staircase, leading into a vast ballroom, and caught the eye of a handsome prince—but then she blinked and crashed down to reality. She reached for the clasp. "I can't. I can't afford it at all."

He leaned forward, elbows on the glass case. "Neither can most people. But I'll make a little bargain with you," he said, reaching behind the case for a piece of paper. It looked like a receipt. "It's just going to stay in the case until next year unless you wear it. It's been part of this collection forever, and it never gets any time out in the sun. And it should! It should be admired! You should wear it. Do it a favor and give it a turn around the dance floor."

"Thank you, but I just said—"

"On the house," he said, scribbling something on the receipt, tearing it off, and adding it to her folio.

"Are you serious?" She shook her head, fingering the necklace. *Millions of euros worth of jewels I don't own.* "Oh, no, I couldn't—"

"Really. It's our pleasure—to have such a beautiful guest as yourself grace these halls. You'll be doing us a favor."

She'd been eyeing her reflection in the mirror again, still touching the necklace she might have been able to afford in her dreams. She couldn't seem to take her eyes off it. Finally, she tore them away and glanced at him. "Well . . . I suppose. If you insist . . ."

He grinned, "I do," handed her the folio and waved, "*Bonne chance!*"

She waved goodbye to him and walked toward the exit. As she did, people gazed at her and beamed, noticing her, and in a good way, something that rarely happened to her anymore. One woman tapped her arm and said, "*Ooo la la,*" and a rather dashing man bowed low to the ground and winked at her. She'd never been the belle of the ball before, but now, she felt like one.

At the checkout desk, she presented her folio and her credit card. There'd soon be a hefty balance on it. She touched the necklace as the lady rang her up. "The gentleman in jewelry said this was on the house?"

The woman read over the folio and smiled, "*Oui. Très jolie.* That was very nice of Monsieur Chevrolet.*"*

"So it's okay?"

She shrugged, "He's head of our concierge, so *oui.*"

Diana let out a sigh of relief. Sure, it was expensive. Silly, possibly. Hedonistic, maybe. But it was okay. This night was what she had come for.

Putting a mental check mark next to agenda item number one, she stepped outside and slipped on the elbow-length gloves she'd been given. One night to have some fun wasn't too much to ask. This was everything, and she couldn't wait.

CHAPTER TWELVE

When Diana had imagined attending a ball at Versailles, she'd imagined strolling the gardens, taking in the fountains, entering gilded halls and rooms of opulence she'd never before seen in her life. But a part of her had also been worried about being that awkward, invisible wallflower of a teenage girl at prom who sat on the bleachers and never got asked to dance.

She didn't have to worry.

From the moment she stepped out of the tent, people were in a jovial, festive mood, calling *Bonsuir* to her. The smiles were endless. The warm summer air was charged with electricity. Each costume was more ornate than the next, and people really seemed to be getting into the parts they were playing. They were clearly just as excited as she was to be there, and it showed.

As she walked down a long straight path through the gardens, admiring a reflection pond surrounded by bright red flowers she didn't know the name of, a young waiter came by with a silver tray of champagne flutes. "*Pour vous, mademoiselle?*"

"Yes, thank you," she said, taking the closest one. The boy was young enough to be her son, but he had those horn-rimmed glasses, just like Stéphane had had. Thirty years ago, on this very day, if she'd have said yes to his invitation, it would have been the beginning of something. He'd said that the ball would kick off their lives together in France.

Now, she felt like she was kicking something else off. Yes, alone, and that made it more frightening, despite her age. But there was far more excitement bubbling in her chest—now . . . and she hadn't even had a sip of her champagne. It felt important, like the beginning of something big and life-altering.

She sipped from the flute and looked around, wondering if Stéphane did, indeed, come to this every year, and if he was here now. Perhaps with his wife and family, but perhaps not. That waiter, with his lanky build and shaggy light-brown hair half in and half out of his collar, could've been *his* son too.

It was all silly, though. Of course, it was a long time ago. But wouldn't it have been funny if just as she'd thought about him, again and again, he'd come to the ball every year, hoping to finally see her too?

She laughed as she sipped more champagne, and the bubbles went up her nose, making her want to sneeze. Things like that only happened in fairy tales and Hallmark movies.

Stop being silly, she scolded herself. *You've seen this place a million times—in pictures. Now you are here. Enjoy it. Take it all in. Make this night absolutely unforgettable . . .*

A young man in a Napoleon costume with a tricorn hat and fake medals and finery—he was certainly as short as the general—and a troupe of his officers sidled down the path toward her. If it weren't for the period costumes, she would've thought they were college frat brothers. They were each carrying big mugs of what must've been draft beer. "Hey, *mademoiselle!*" the man called, whistling at her. He sang, badly, "I'm finally facing my Waterloo."

She rolled her eyes, even though something about his silliness was charming.

He jogged toward her. "Take a picture with us? *S'il vous plait?*"

She nodded and crossed over that path to them, then realized she hadn't yet taken any pictures with her own phone. She got in the center of the men and smiled as they snapped picture after picture. She handed them her phone, and they took pictures for her too. "You sound British?" she said to Napoleon.

He nodded, "That's right. Me and mates just come over here for this party. You American?"

"Yes. I've always wanted to go to this, ever since I first heard of it a long time ago. It took me a while to get here, though."

"Well," he took her fingertips and pressed a very wet and slightly unpleasant kiss into the back of her hand, leaving a lip-print on the back of her glove. "Enjoy the fantasy!"

She smiled as they staggered away, weaving in and out of the crowd and nearly spilling beer on just about everyone they met. As she looked around, she realized it was true. The clientele leaned toward the millennial side. Maybe that was all the type of guest this kind of extravagant party attracted—young foreigners who used it as an excuse to booze it up. There were a few older couples, but most were definitely closer in age to Diana's children.

No matter, she told herself, as her stomach growled under her corset. She'd been too nervous to eat much all day, but now she was starving. *Time for the buffet. At least I can get a good meal out of it.*

The pre-party dinner buffet was outdoors on one of the many lawns. The line of food seemed to stretch on forever, and the tangy scent of citrus and the savory smell of cooked ham wafted to greet her, even before she'd walked around the privet hedge surrounding the dining area. There were round tables set up upon the lawn, and people were eating with plastic forks and paper napkins. *Not exactly authentic, but it beats eating with my hands!* she thought, going to the end of the line and taking a paper plate from the pile.

The website had advertised a "sumptuous buffet fit for royalty," and the food on the serving trays, at least in appearance, lived up to that. A *salade niçoise* and *escargot* appetizer, along with all the French favorites—*bouillabaisse, cassoulet, beef bourguignon*—were there for the taking, as well as carving stations full of large cuts of fresh meat and plenty of sides like roasted carrots and *gratin dauphinois*. The dessert table was full of treats, including miniature containers of crème brulee and pots de crème, and there was a station making fresh crepes to order.

Let them eat cake! She thought to herself, smiling as she took her silverware. *And I will. A lot of it. Until my corset bursts at the seams.*

She'd just started to ladle a helping of *coq au vin* onto her plate when she looked up, across the buffet, to the balustrade of a garden folly.

Diana's breath left her.

There he was.

He was wearing a blue velvet waistcoat with tails, trousers that were buttoned at the knee, and stockings, which of course was the fashion of that time. A tricorn hat completed the costume. Though he was facing away from her, she knew it in an instant. Stéphane had had a physique that most men would've killed for—he was tall and athletic, lean but substantial. She'd especially loved the look of his posterior, the way he filled out his jeans. Though many men these days would have taken issue with donning stockings, Stéphane wouldn't have, for good reason—he made even stockings and the frilly blouses of the time look masculine. He wore the ensemble—it didn't wear him.

This man made all the other men, though they were all dressed in very similar finery, look like court jesters.

She stared at him as he strode across the balustrade, hands clasped behind him, like he often used to do while strolling from class to class at NYU, in an easy way, like he had not a care in the world. At the edge of the railing, he met a waiter and, after pausing to push his glasses up on the bridge of his nose, took a glass of champagne. He nodded cordially in thanks and said something to the waiter, who smiled as if his day had been made. That was Stéphane. Always excessively polite—to everyone.

Her heart twisted. She only realized she'd forgotten to breath when she began to feel a dizziness swarming her head.

Suddenly, someone nudged her elbow. *"Excusez-moi,"* an elderly woman next to her said, motioning with a wrinkled finger. Diana looked down and realized her hand was still fastened around the handle of the ladle, and the helping of food on her paper plate was in danger of running onto her dress.

"Oh, I'm sorry. Here," she said, shifting the handle into the woman's grasp and stepping out of line. Eyes still planted on Stéphane as he weaved his way among the guests, she drifted toward him, her feet moving almost entirely of their own volition—as if she were a puppet on a string.

She approached the stairs and realized she couldn't both hold her food and lift her enormous skirt to ascend at the same time, so she set the plate down on a pedestal. Food was the last thing on her mind now.

Darkness was falling, and the second the sun slipped behind the trees. Someone somewhere must've flipped a switch because the gardens lit up in a gorgeous display. Millions of little white fairy lights dangled from the trees, and spotlights illuminated the statues. But Diana barely noticed it. She grabbed her skirts and floated up the stairs, thinking of the last thing Stéphane had said to her all those years ago.

Je t'adore, mi amor. We will be together again, in Paris!

So what if it had taken a few extra decades? Now, after all those years of wondering "what if," it felt like a lifelong dream was finally about to come true.

CHAPTER THIRTEEN

When Diana reached the top of the steps, she hesitated and took a deep breath. Her pulse was pounding in her ears, and all she could hear was her blood, swishing through her veins. She felt flushed, dizzy, but the hands she wrung in front of her were cold as ice. Goosebumps appeared on her chest, in that tender skin above her cleavage that wasn't used to seeing the light of day. She felt like she might faint, but she also never felt more alive. More like this was destiny at play, finally interceding to make all of her dreams a reality.

What should I say? She wondered as she stood there, watching him at the balustrade, enjoying his champagne. *"Hello, Stéphane, it has been a while."* or, *"Hey, stranger!"* or *"Do you even remember me?"*

What difference did it make what she opened with? If he loved her, he loved her. True soul mates never simply forgot each other, did they?

She just had the feeling that this was a monumental moment, one that would shape the entire rest of her life. Make the night truly unforgettable. And she wanted to make it perfect.

Oh, stop. Nothing in your life has ever been perfect. But it has worked out.

She was overthinking things. As usual. She just needed to move.

So she stormed forward and tugged on his elbow. *"Bons—"*

She froze when the man turned around.

The first thing she noticed was that the glasses were all wrong. They were square-framed, not circular. *So he changed the style,* she thought at first, but then she took notice of his long, angular hooked nose. His beady eyes, beneath an unfortunate thickly gray unibrow that even the black mask under his glasses could not hide. His pointed chin. When he smiled at her, he bared teeth the color of aged paper with a deeply pronounced gap between the top front ones. *Stéphane had a smile like a toothpaste commercial.* "Yes?" he said.

NO, every pore of her body screamed.

She took a step away. Then another. "Sorry. I thought you were someone else," she muttered, then put her head down and tried to escape. She attempted to scurry off, but the dress made that impossible. She tripped and stumbled her way across the marble balcony until she came to the portico outside the palace.

When she was out of his sight, she sighed. Of course, she'd just been silly. How stupid to foster a fantasy of someone who'd likely forgotten her decades ago?

People were starting to go inside for the ball portion of the event. Diana looked around, contemplating whether she should go back to the buffet line and drown her sorrows in a big vat of *crème brulee.* Yes. Sure, she'd give the corset a workout, but how ridiculous was she? Did she really think she'd find love here, after all these years? The least she could do was eat her money's worth of those sumptuous French pastries and desserts.

She lifted her skirts, about to make a bee-line for the buffet, when a voice behind her said, *"Excusez-moi de vous déranger. . ."* Excuse me, sorry to bother you . . .

She whirled so suddenly she felt her corset nearly rip at her ribcage. Grabbing hold of it, she looked up into the most intense green eyes she'd ever seen, framed by a simple black mask, which only seemed to make them more striking. The man in front of her was tall, wearing a red waistcoat with an abundance of brass buttons on the hem, his hand tucked into it as if he were a distinguished gentleman posing for a portrait. He wasn't wearing one of those ridiculous wigs. And there was a slight bit of gray peppering his temples, but other than that, he had a thick dark head of hair, a few curls of which tumbled rakishly into his tanned forehead.

She stared, speechless.

The man continued with, *"Mais j'ai un problème."* I have a problem. *"Pouvez-vous m'aider?"* Can you help me?

She kept staring for a few moments too long—until a silence crept in. He tilted his head, apparently waiting for an answer, and she realized that this was when she was expected to respond. She let out a girlish giggle and winced. "Uh . . . *oui,"* she said, her entire body now matching the red of the rubies in her necklace. "But I don't speak French very well. *Je parle un peu français. Parlez lentement, s'il vous plait?"* I speak but a little French. Speak slowly, please.

"Ah, you speak English. You are American?" he asked in perfect English with only a hint of an accent, just as Stéphane had had.

She nodded, hoping he wouldn't hold it against her, "You said you had a problem, *monsieur*?"

He bared his teeth in a perfect toothpaste-commercial smile, one that was neither lecherous or insincere. "Yes, indeed I do, *chéri*. I have met a beautiful woman, an angel," he said, his eyes never leaving hers, "And I am wondering how to go about asking such a lovely creature to come down from the heavens and dance with me?"

"Oh!" Diana blurted dreamily. For a moment, she wondered, *Is he really speaking to me?* But the look in his eyes left little doubt for that. She pushed a curl that had fallen forward behind her collarbone and said, "I haven't even been in the palace yet."

"Well, by all means, allow me to escort you," he said, offering her his elbow. "It will be my sincerest pleasure."

She hesitated. "I should warn you . . . I don't know the steps of any of those country dances."

He chuckled. "In the ballroom, we'll be waltzing. You do waltz?"

"Oh, okay. A bit," she said, only slightly relieved. When was the last time she'd danced a waltz? It had to have been at her wedding reception. Evan had never cared much for dancing, and hadn't been very good at it. So the two of them never tripped the light fantastic.

However, this man? This man looked like the type of man who played polo. Who scrutinized the wine list at fancy restaurants. Who owned more than one tuxedo. Who waltzed for fun.

She took his offered elbow, and he walked her toward the magnificent arch of double doors into the building. It was a grand entrance, even though it wasn't the main one. The second she went through, she inhaled the scent of cinnamon and cloves. The air was sparkling with excitement, the candles and chandeliers fully lit. Diana gaped up at one of them that had to have been bigger than her bedroom back on Long Island. "Golly," she breathed.

He laughed, "That is a common reaction."

She gazed at the tapestries and paintings adorning the rich red velvet wallpaper, the gilded fixtures and sconces, the marble floors. The hallway was an explosion of color—even the ceiling a work of art though it almost felt as if it were miles above her. Everywhere, there was something amazing to see. "You have been here many times?"

"*Oui,*" he said with a smile. "My family goes way back to the age of the French monarchy. Ours served the last king."

"Really?" *Like Stéphane's family.* Yes, he was different, but she couldn't help wondering everything about him, just like she'd been with her first love. "I'm Diana."

He stopped, gently took her hand, and kissed it. As he did, his eyes never left hers. "I am Lucien Beauchamp, cómte de Monteil de Saint-Quentin. You can call me Luc. It is a great pleasure to meet you, the most beautiful woman in the palace tonight."

The goosebumps everywhere on her body became mountains. "Oh."

He then extended his arm to her, leading her to the great ballroom as if he'd traveled these halls many times before. Even so, he stopped to allow her to see everything and offered tidbits of helpful information, like a tour guide. He stopped in front of a picture of a lady in a white wig and a beautiful blue-gray gown, holding a delicate rose. "There is a portrait of the lady herself, Marie Antoinette. One of many in the palace. There are over 60,000 pieces of artwork on the grounds. No doubt you saw the many Greco-Roman sculptures outside?"

"I did," she said, pausing to look at an elaborate gilded clock. "I found the Fountain of Apollo breathtaking."

"Yes, it is. It was much less so during the rule of Louis XIII. His son, the Sun King, added the gilded lead representing Apollo on his chariot, during his rule. The work of the sculptor Jean-Baptiste Tuby is quite magnificent." He pointed to the clock. "That clock was designed by Claude-Simeon Passemant, clockmaker extraordinaire, who is responsible for many of the timepieces in the palace. The rococo style is obviously evident, being a favorite of Louis XIV."

"I see," she said, even though she really didn't. "You know so much about this palace."

"Yes. It's like a second home to me," he said, guiding her to a massive foyer. From there, the lilting music of a waltz filled the air. He led her though a set of massive double doors into the ballroom, the legendary Hall of Mirrors.

She gasped. It was nothing like what she'd imagined from the pictures. None of that could ever do it justice. It was so much vaster and more extravagant than anything her mind had conjured up. The mirrors and gold-inlaid walls seemed to stretch on forever. Yes, the Sun King had liked things bright, and this was brilliantly so—as if the walls were on fire. The chandeliers up above were enormous. The entire room, and all of the people inside, seemed to sparkle as though they were fireworks themselves.

"Come," he said with a gentle smile, and swept her onto the dance floor. He placed one hand at the small of her back and clasped her hand with a gloved hand of his own.

She'd been wondering how she'd waltz—and especially how she'd manage with all that fabric around her legs—but it turned out, she needn't have worried. Luc was an adept leader and swept her around the floor as if he'd been leading women across dance floors all his life. She'd been worried about stepping on his toes, but he was so light on his feet that it almost felt like they were soaring. All the while, he kept his emerald eyes on hers, so she had no choice but to gaze deep into his.

"Tell me something about yourself, beautiful Diana from America," he said.

"Oh. There's not much to tell. I live in New York. I used to work for a cosmetics company, but I'm in the middle of a divorce and decided to take a year off to explore Europe."

When she mentioned the divorce, his interest only seemed to grow. "Ah. How could any man ever decide to let you go?"

She fought the blush climbing on her cheeks, "We had a good marriage. A long one. I have no regrets. My only one—I'm taking care of now, with this trip."

"And how are you liking it?"

He suddenly spun her, and amazingly, she didn't fall on her backside. When she turned around and faced him again, he took her hand in his, dragging her up to meet him. She gushed dreamily, "It's amazing." Then she realized she sounded like a twelve-year-old and added, "Actually, I haven't seen much. I've only just arrived."

"And it is your first time in Paris?" When she nodded, he said, "I should hope you have someone to show you around?"

"No, I came here alone."

"That is a shame, that a lovely lady like yourself is condemned to travel through Paris alone," he said, but his smile grew.

"I don't mind it. But I admit it would be nice to have someone to show me around. Someone in the know."

He chuckled, "Perhaps, we can arrange that."

A shiver went down her spine. No, this wasn't Stéphane, but maybe . . . She squelched those childish thoughts before she could allow them to take root and grow. "And you? Are you here alone?"

"I am, this time. Of course, it is not my first time, but it is, unfortunately, my first time alone."

She waited for him to say more, maybe that he'd just been divorced too. But he didn't. She could feel his hand in hers, and it didn't have a ring on it.

He broke from her eyes just long enough to glance downward. "I see you are wearing one of the palace's collection."

"Yes. I wasn't going to. But they insisted on it. They can be persuasive."

"I imagine so. It is a beautiful piece, but truthfully, your beauty eclipses it. You do not need it."

Her cheeks felt hot again. The waltz ended, and as the last violin note hung in the air, people applauded mildly. She reached into her purse and pulled out the fan she'd stashed there, and when she opened it, realized he was staring at her, a pensive look on his face. The blush came full-on now, so she waved the fan in her face. "I'm sure you've been to many of these, so you know how things work. What do we do, now?"

He chuckled softly, "Well, it depends on who you are. Most of society—the good ones, anyway—will sit around here and prattle on about dull topics all evening. But the daring ones?" He arched his brow in a mysterious way, "They would do something else."

Now she was curious, "What, exactly?"

"The daring ones would take the chance and meet on the balcony, right out those doors. It is dark there, and there are plenty of little nooks and alcoves where people can get away from the crowds. They'd meet out there under the cover of darkness . . ."

She stared at him. Was he really suggesting a tryst? No, a *rendezvous?* With a man she'd just met? "What do you—"

He silenced her by putting a finger gently to her lips, "I'll go now. Wait five minutes, and then join me?" He leaned over and placed a sweet peck on her forehead, and smiled a coy smile, "Five minutes. Don't forget."

And then he left her, weaving his way through the crowded dance floor. She watched him climb the stairs and disappear, her heart beating like mad.

She only realized that the dancing had started again when someone bumped into her. Everyone else had begun to move, except her. Quickly, she grabbed her skirts and made her way around the waltzing couples, trying to escape. All the while, thoughts swirled in her head.

A *rendezvous.*

Evan hadn't exactly been romantic in that way. And she hadn't even kissed any man other than Evan since . . . *Stéphane.* To say she was rusty was an understatement.

But she'd come for an adventure. For something new. And while it might not have been her college boyfriend, it was her dream come true.

This was going to be an evening she remembered the rest of her life. And she was going to make the most of it. *Make this night unforgettable . . .*

This time, no regrets.

CHAPTER FOURTEEN

Diana escaped down the long foyer, rushing past gilded wall panels, priceless works of art, and couples in their elegant costumes, and found the public restrooms. When she was safely in there, away from the ball, she let out the breath she'd been holding, stood in front of the mirror, fanning her flushed face madly.

Oh my god. I'm really doing this. With a man I just met. Am I crazy? No, you're not. You're not overthinking it. You're not going to let this opportunity pass you by. You're going to go for it. This is really happening.

She looked unlike herself. Younger, different, and it wasn't just the makeup. She felt a youthful giddiness inside she hadn't felt since . . . well, she couldn't remember. Probably before she married Evan.

Reaching into her bag, she reapplied her lipstick, dusted powder on her shiny nose and forehead, and straightened the gold mask around her eyes. Then she felt her earrings and made sure they were properly clipped on. Her chest was flushed. Her eyes went down to the sparkling diamond, resting just above her cleavage. She started to pull up the lace trim so she could be more respectable, then stopped herself. Everything was covered. She looked good. Darn good. And there was nothing wrong with using a little sex appeal.

So instead of trying to cover up, Diana ran her hands along the sides of her ribcage and lifted her breasts in the corset so that they were higher. Now, the diamond's bottom dipped almost into her cleavage. She turned to the side, held her shoulders back, and inspected herself. *Not bad. You almost look like one of the daring ones.*

Which reminded her . . .

It had likely been at least four minutes since she'd left Luc. If she didn't hurry, he might think she chickened out and leave. She imagined him in his dashing mask, leaning against a pillar, waiting in the darkness for her, and her heart thudded. This was like something out of one of those tawdry bodice-ripper romance novels. She could almost imagine the back-cover blurb: *a chance encounter with a masked nobleman changed her life forever . . .*

The door opened. A few ladies came into the stuffy bathroom just then and started their preening, so Diana quickly made her exit. Every step she took on the marble floor echoed hollowly in her ears. Trying to keep her breathing even, she backtracked to the doors Luc had pointed to, and slipped out through the first set of double doors to the vestibule.

From there, she could see the balcony through the next set of doors. The railing was adorned in white fairy lights, but just as Luc had promised, the vast marble portico was full of little nooks and alcoves made by various fountains, sculptures, and pruned hedges. A few people milled about, and shadows were everywhere, fooling her eyes. She hesitated there, wondering where among all the hidden places she'd find him. What if he was only teasing her? What if he'd never intended to meet with her?

Don't be silly. You're both adults. He's not some young, silly man, playing games.

She swallowed, thinking of what Lily would say: *You're going to go out in the dark with some stranger, Mom? Some stranger who could be an axe-murderer. Really smart! Aren't you the one who made me carry a rape whistle everywhere I went in college?*

That was true. She had always been more concerned over her children, her family, than she had been about herself. But really, when in the past had she done *anything* even remotely daring? This trip to Europe was supposed to be just that . . . a chance to break free, to experience *different.*

And Luc certainly was different.

Besides, as an adult, there is nothing wrong with spending some time getting acquainted with another single man.

She stopped with her hand on the shining brass door handle and peered through the window, trying to make him out among the other costumed men. Though the colors of their finery was slightly different, out in the darkness, they all looked rather the same. But Luc . . . Luc had a build very much like Stéphane's, one that was hard to miss.

She squinted some more, and after a few moments, a sinking feeling began to pool in her stomach. He wasn't there.

Of course, he's there. The balcony is huge, probably, and you can't see all of it. He's out there, somewhere, waiting for you. You just need to take the first step and find him. Find your destiny!

She took a deep breath and was about to throw open the door when suddenly, a drunken caravan of young men and women, hooting loudly, rushed past her as if she was invisible. They threw open the door, arms linked, rushed out into the night.

Diana whirled and tried to scurry away from them, but her skirts made a quick escape impossible. The man at the tail end of the procession, a slovenly bald red-goateed man in a jester's costume that was too small to hold in all of his massive hairy pale stomach, noticed her at the last moment. He held out a glass of champagne to her, spilling it everywhere, and slurred, "Hey, *mademoiselle,* come with us!"

She shook her head, but he kept reaching for her, and as he did, she noticed the sweat stains on the armpits of his costume. The costume department was going to have *lots* of fun with that one. They'd probably have to incinerate it after he got done with it. "Come on! Please! Make my dreams come true!"

"Oh no, that's—"

Before she could step away, he grabbed for her. He clasped onto her hand just as the rest of his crew yanked him forward. Diana, still holding onto the door, lost her balance and went sprawling on her hands and knees on the top step, hopelessly tangled in the pile of her dress. By then, the drunken fools were already at the bottom of the staircase and rushing into the night.

"Sorry!" the jester called with a mighty guffaw, disappearing from view.

"Just . . . *whatever,*" Diana mumbled, looking down at all the silk surrounding her, making sure she hadn't ruined the fabric during her fall. It looked okay. No tears or champagne stains. When she tried to get to her feet, her bare foot touched the cold marble, and she realized she'd lost her shoe. "Yes, this is just the kind of Cinderella experience I'd expect to have."

She was so busy trying to find her lost heel, fishing her hands under the pile of fabric, that she barely noticed the door behind her opening and closing. She found the shoe somewhere on the top step and slipped into it as someone said, *"Est-ce que je peux vous aider?"* Can I help you?

A man in a dark mask with golden swirls around the eye holes and two very pronounced, arched eyebrows that made it look like he was perpetually questioning everything—stood in front of her. He took her hand and lifted her to standing. *"il n'y a pas de mal."*

She wasn't sure what that meant, but she was too flustered to care. "Thanks," she said, brushing her skirts off and scanning the area. Now she was outdoors, and it was chilly but not unpleasant, and somewhere out there, *hopefully,* a man was waiting for her to make a thirty-year dream come true.

*

She rushed down the steps and onto the balcony, looking around. Once she was on the balcony, she realized just how big it was. It stretched on like a football field and was full of statues and garden sculptures and fountains. Sure enough, there were several couples, sitting on benches or the edge of fountains, making out. Not one of them was Luc. In fact, all of them seemed very young.

Because people your age don't do silly things like this, a little voice inside her said, her spirits threatening to plummet, but she pushed that away. *Make this night unforgettable!*

She walked up and down the marble squares, still searching. He'd seemed so sincere. Had he really just led her out there to tease her? What kind of adult man did that?

No. He will be there, Diana. And you WILL make this night unforgettable!

She continued to waffle between hopelessness and excitement as she rounded a massive fountain with a Greek statue of a naked man and woman embracing in the throes of passion. It only served to make her more eager to see Luc. Not that she cared much about passion, but the attention Luc had paid her had awoken something in her . . . she missed the company of men. She had to admit—she really did.

Maybe he's running late. Well, I don't care. I'm waiting here until he comes, and I will not feel guilty about it. I am going to make this night one to remember.

She walked to the edge of the balcony, listening to the sound of the crickets, which was met only sporadically by waltz music every time the door to the inside opened.

In a Greek tragedy, this would've been where the heroine threw herself over the side in despair. She walked another few steps and stopped when she saw a half-empty glass of champagne, sitting abandoned on the marble railing.

It shouldn't have concerned her. After all, the champagne was flowing, and flutes were everywhere. Someone had probably just left it there.

But something about it struck her. In the minimal light, she could see the bubbles rising to the surface of the champagne, as if it had been poured not very long ago. She went over to the balcony and rested her elbows on the thick marble railing, then stared up at the night sky. Behind her, the lilting waltz played, and occasionally, someone laughed or shouted. But here, it was peaceful. There was a line of trees in the far distance, and beyond that, the lights of Paris spread out. In the middle, the Eiffel Tower rose up, lit like a candle.

Gorgeous. A beautiful night, and a beautiful sight to sit and take in with someone else. Particularly a man who adored her.

She sighed, thinking of Lily and Bea and wondering if they were right. She'd spent her whole life trying to temper their expectations and understand reality. When as a toddler, Bea had wanted to grow up to be a turtle, she'd told her that wouldn't be possible. When Lily, as a girl in grade school, said she hated boys and wanted to marry her dad, who was the only perfect man on earth, Diana had shot that down too. She'd tempered all their crazy whims, talked them down to reality. Why couldn't she seem to do the same for herself? Some dreams and wishes were simply foolish, childish, and should never be allowed to come true.

Maybe this was one of them. Maybe, this was the universe's wake-up call.

"Oh, girls," she whispered aloud. "If you saw me now, you'd probably be embarrassed for me."

She reached for the glass of champagne and went to pour it over the side of the balcony. When she looked over, she was surprised to see how high up they were—at least three stories. She scanned lower and was just about to pour the champagne over the side when she saw a faint outline, below. The head in profile, the shoulders bent strangely, the arms and legs sprawled out in unnatural, almost ninety-degree angles.

Diana blinked. If that hadn't been a wake-up call before, this *definitely* was it.

Because that faint silhouette below her looked an awful lot like a dead body.

CHAPTER FIFTEEN

Diana screamed.

She'd never been one for hysterics, but right now, she couldn't help it. The more she looked at it, the more engrained into her head it became. Twisted, mangled, unnatural . . . and dead. She'd never seen a dead body before, but though she wanted to look away, she simply couldn't stop staring.

One hand on the railing, one hand clutching the champagne glass that wasn't hers, she felt dizzy—like the world was a spinning carousel and there was no way to get off. She was vaguely aware of people rushing to her assistance, asking what was the matter, but she couldn't speak.

They soon found out the problem, anyway. More and more people began to arrive, crowding around her and peering over the railing, pointing. A few appeared on the ground beside the dead body, looking up at the balcony to try to ascertain where he'd come from. Some women screamed, like she had. Voices and chatter rose around her, tearing at the perfect silence that had once fallen over the night.

As she stared, unable to rip her eyes from the sight, she noticed certain things. The coat he was wearing was not black; it was midnight blue. The mask had fallen off him, but it was simple and black. The man had a lot of dark wavy hair.

It was him. Luc.

A thousand thoughts twisted in her head. He'd invited her out here. He'd come to meet with her. And then . . . then . . . then what?

What had happened in those five minutes?

Something terribly wrong.

Suddenly, someone put an arm around her and said, "Come with me, dear."

She tore herself away from the grisly scene and followed that person like a child, her body trembling. The good Samaritan guided Diana to a bench, where she sat, holding the glass of champagne.

Without thinking, she brought the glass to her lips and downed the whole thing in one gulp.

A second later, she pulled back and winced. *It's very likely you just drank a dead man's champagne. This is a new low for you, Diana.*

She set the flute beside her and hugged herself, rubbing her arms, but that didn't seem to do any good. She was still shivering.

She blinked when she realized someone was sitting beside her, talking to her. It was an older lady in a blue satin gown with a massive wig, done up to look exactly like Marie Antoinette had she lived to an older age. The woman stroked her hand and said in an accent she couldn't quite place, "I know this must've been a shock for you, dear. Did you see what happened?"

Diana shook her head. "No . . . I saw nothing."

"Are you sure?"

No. She wasn't sure of everything. All the sights and sounds around her had been overwhelming to begin with, and now, they were a thousand times more so. Even though she was seated, the balcony around her was still spinning, and she couldn't breathe. Marie Antoinette fanned her face, but the breeze only served to distract Diana more.

Was she sure? Definitely not. In fact, she couldn't even remember what she'd been doing in the minutes before she'd come outside. All the events from the day seemed to swirl together into one jumbled mess.

She shook her head as more and more people began to rush to the scene. Some of them were uniformed security guards. Some people were shocked, and others seemed to think it was just a part of the playacting that was going on. Whatever it was, it was chaos . . . so many people, all speaking at once. Diana closed her eyes and tried to find her Zen, just as the woman beside her began to speak loudly over her head.

"Here, dear! You're looking for the person who discovered him? Right here. This lady, over here!"

Diana opened her eyes in time to see about twenty heads swing toward her. A short man in an overcoat and moustache broke through and started to speak to her in mile-a-minute French. Diana's first thought was *Inspector Clouseau?* She opened her mouth to ask him to speak slower, but nothing came out. Her vocal cords had withered from the strain of all the screaming she'd done.

"I'm sorry, dear," the woman next to her said, still patting her hand. "I don't think the poor love speaks any French. I think she's in shock. She was jabbering on in English when I found her."

I was? Diana thought. She couldn't remember any of that, either. The only thing in the center of her mind, almost in a spotlight, was the outline of the dead body on the concrete below.

The man sat down beside her and flipped her his credentials. All she saw, though, was the dead body. He smelled vaguely of tobacco, a scent she got a lot of in her nostrils since she was close to hyperventilating. "I am Lieutenant Pierre Bayans, of the *Prefecture de Police* of Paris. You found the body?"

She nodded, rubbing her hands furiously over her bare arms to warm up.

"Oh, the poor thing's clearly upset. Do you have to do this to her now?" the older woman said. "She's—"

"*Excusez-moi*, Madame, would you be so kind as to get the lady a cup of tea from inside?" he said brusquely.

The woman hesitated as if she didn't want to miss a bit of the action. "Well . . . yes. I suppose." She stood up and headed away.

"*Merci beaucoup,*" the lieutenant said, not looking up. "And what is your name?"

"Diana," she whispered. "Diana St. James."

"You're American? And you were attending the ball? Alone?"

She nodded.

"Why don't you start from the beginning and tell me what you saw?" he said, getting his notepad at the ready.

"I honestly didn't see much at all. I came outside, and I didn't see anyone, and I went to the railing and looked over. And then I saw him. That was all."

"That is all?" he asked. She could tell by the way he wrote absolutely nothing in his notebook beside her name that her account was just as unhelpful as she'd thought. "You didn't see anyone?"

"Not a soul," she murmured, but the moment she said it, images from before the discovery shook loose in her head and came to the forefront. "Well . . . I saw a few couples together, on different parts of the balcony, but I didn't get a good look at them. And—"

She stopped. Yes, now, more and more was coming back to her.

"Yes?" he prompted.

"There were some younger, rather drunk people, who ran out onto the balcony before I did. But they headed a different direction from where . . ." She pointed to the other side of the balcony. After that, no more flashes of inspiration struck her. Again, images of Luc's dead body crowded out all calm, logical thought. "That's all."

"Had you seen the victim before?"

She stiffened. She knew she should probably tell the truth, but wouldn't that make her a suspect? The first thing out of her mouth was, "I . . . don't think so." Then, she thought better of it. There was a good chance someone would've have seen the two of them, dancing together. The police would put two and two together and wonder why she'd lied. "I mean . . . I didn't really get a good look at the body. I danced with a man in the ballroom. It might've been him."

"This man you danced with . . ." He asked, now writing something in his book. "Who was he? Do you see him anywhere, now?"

She looked around, all the while knowing she *wouldn't* see him, because right now, he was lying dead on a concrete patio. "I think he said his name was Luc?"

"And what was he wearing?"

"A blue velvet coat with brass buttons and a black mask."

He nodded. "Well, that fits the description of the victim. We haven't identified him. Can you tell me anything about what you two talked about?"

"He told me he's been to Versailles a lot. He described a lot of the artwork to me. And then we waltzed, and . . ." she winced. Now, their rendezvous didn't just sound silly. It could likely get her in a lot of trouble. "Well . . . it must've been an accident, right? Maybe he had too much to drink, and he slipped . . ."

"Did he seem that way, when you spoke to him?"

Oh, he'd seemed a lot of things, to Diana. Handsome. Dazzling. A dream come true. But *dead*? It was almost too much, too horrible to believe. "Huh?"

"Did he seem drunk?" he pressed.

She gnawed on her lip and shook her head. "No. He was coherent. But . . ."

"I brought you your tea, dear!" a voice called from behind her, as the woman came back, saving the day with a tiny china teacup and saucer, which she set on Diana's lap.

"Thank you," Diana said, taking a sip. It burned her mouth, but she didn't even care.

The lieutenant growled at the interruption, but that didn't stop Old Marie Antoinette from standing there expectantly as if she wanted to be included in the conversation, "Oh, it's the least I can do, love."

The lieutenant looked up at her and scratched at his cheek near the end of his dark moustache. She seemed to have rooted herself to the spot.

"*S'il vous plait, madame* . . . wait over there while I finish with this witness," he sounded firm, but not angry, as if he was used to dealing with busybodies.

She frowned but eventually did as he said. The lieutenant leaned forward. "You were about to say something about the victim? After you waltzed, what happened?"

"Yes . . . after we waltzed," she said, looking down into her tea. "After we waltzed, he went out the double doors to the balcony, and I went to the restroom."

It was the truth, really. With just one small omission . . . that he'd invited her to accompany him outside. That she *should* have been with him at the moment he died. That maybe if she had not questioned herself and headed out there right away, he might still be alive . . .

She clenched her teeth at the thought. Was this her fault?

"And you didn't see him again until you found him dead?"

She nodded.

"You're an American?"

"Yes."

"Where are you staying, and for how long?"

"*Le Bonne Auberge.* I had planned to stay in Paris for the next three days. Then—"

"All right, Ms. St. James," he said, slapping his notebook closed. "As far as I can tell, you're probably the last person to have seen him before he died, so I'd like you to stay close. Do you understand?"

She nodded. Yes. She understood.

He didn't say as much, but she knew exactly what it meant. Even though she hadn't told him she was due to meet Luc for a tryst, she was still a suspect. So that probably meant—forget the sightseeing, the carefree stopping by cafes for a croissant, the dreams of a romance with a dashing French gentleman. She was going to have to spend the rest of her time with Inspector Clouseau following her around, putting her every move under a magnifying glass.

And forget about checking out of *Le Bonne Auberge.* Right now, it was *Le Bonne Prison.*

She polished off her tea, and though her limbs were now feeling a little warmer, she couldn't help wondering, *Really, what else can possibly go wrong?* It felt like ages since she'd rolled up to Versailles in the bus, since she'd put on this constricting corset and heavy gown, since that flamboyant French salesman had draped the massive necklace over her chest. It seemed like . . .

Suddenly, she realized something was off, and it wasn't just the whole dead-Frenchman thing. Something was wrong.

When she brought a hand up to her chest and all she felt was her madly beating heart, she knew what it was. She fumbled about, feeling her clammy skin, the hollow of her throat, each collarbone. But there was nothing else. Nothing at all.

She screamed again, this time even louder than before.

CHAPTER SIXTEEN

Diana was hardly aware of all the people staring at her now, wondering where the *next* dead body was. She kept touching the bare skin of her chest, hoping against hope that the missing necklace would magically appear. She pushed aside the loose-hanging locks of hair on at her neck, wondering if it'd somehow gotten caught in them. Then she pulled away the front of her dress slightly and peeked in her cleavage, hoping it'd somehow fallen in, not that the corset would've allowed for such a thing.

No luck.

Her earrings? She reached up and touched each lobe. Thankfully, they were still there. She unclipped them and tucked them carefully into her purse.

After that, she meandered about aimlessly, keeping her eyes peeled to the ground, trying to retrace her steps over the night, but she could barely remember the last two minutes, much less the entire night. When was the last time she'd had it on?

The answer to that came to her right away. When she'd gone to the bathroom, she'd had it on. She'd straightened it in the mirror.

Good. That's good, she thought to herself, her heart beating double time now. *I must've lost it sometime from the time I left the bathroom until now. If it's anywhere, it's got to be around here.*

But the balcony was now *packed* with people, all wanting to get in on the excitement of the murder. If she had lost the necklace, it was likely someone would've noticed it by now. And all she could do was hope that whoever discovered it was honest enough to turn it in to lost and found. Did they have lost and found? Or would they just turn it into a policeman since there were now plenty of those around?

She scanned around, and that was when she realized people were still looking at her curiously. A lot of them. A couple of them were policemen. Almost on cue, one of them went to Inspector Clouseau, whispered something, and pointed. He started to walk over to her.

Oh, please don't, she thought, turning and starting to head off. The last thing she needed was to have to talk to him in the middle of her breakdown.

"*Mademoiselle* St. James?"

Her body tensed. She froze, plastered an *I'm okay! Really, I am!* smile on her face, and turned around. "Yes?"

"Is anything the matter?"

Of course. She wasn't fooling anyone. She *did* look kind of insane. And maybe even a little guilty. Because how much did that man at the jewelry counter say the necklace was worth?

A million dollars.

A million freaking dollars.

She had a retirement account. A substantial one. One she thought would last her until her well into her golden years, not be drained during one night's indiscretion. *Would* she be on the hook for it? Weren't things like that insured?

Her breath hitched as that thought flitted through her mind. "Ye-es." *That was really smooth, Diana.* She composed herself and tried again: "Why wouldn't it be? I mean, other than finding that dead body. I'm a little rattled, of course. But I'll be fine. Thanks."

He nodded at her, still studying her suspiciously, so she turned and walked away. *Well, that was awkward. Now I'm not just a suspect. I'm officially Suspect Number One.*

She headed toward the doors to the palace, trying as hard as she could to be nonchalant while her heart was exploding in her chest. She could feel his eyes on her back, cutting into her shoulder blades. As she walked, her eyes darted around, taking in every possible inch of the balcony she could without drawing more suspicion her way.

No necklace.

The second she rounded the fountain, she looked over her shoulder. She was out of his view. Heaving a sigh of relief, she peeked in the bubbling water of the fountain. In a flower bed. Did a circle around a Greco-Roman sculpture, hoping to find the necklace tucked in some hidden nook there. She crouched low, which wasn't easy in that dress, and looked under a bush, hoping someone had kicked it under there.

Nothing.

This is not good. Not good at all.

As she was standing from her crouch, someone extended a hand to help her up. She took it and came face to face with the Marie

Antoinette busybody who'd gotten her tea. "Are you looking for something in particular?" she asked.

She nodded. "I just seem to have misplaced something."

"Ah. What?"

Diana patted her chest. "My necklace. Do you happen to see it anywhere?"

"Oh. Poor thing." She started to scan the ground around them. "What did it look like?"

People were beginning to clear out of the balcony, leaving the smooth marble floor empty, glistening in the moonlight. It was easier now to see that the necklace wasn't there. "It had rubies, and a giant, eighteen-carat diamond," she said, her spirits sinking. "It's pretty big. You can't miss it."

The woman's eyes snapped to her. "Oh, my. That sounds . . . expensive."

Don't remind me. "It's not mine, of course. It belongs to Versailles. They just let me borrow it from the rental station."

Now the woman looked truly alarmed. "And you lost it?"

Diana gnawed on her lip. "I had it, before I came out here. I don't know . . ."

"It's possible someone turned it in to authorities at the main entrance," the woman said. "I can ask for you?"

Diana shook her head, "No, thank you. I'll do it myself."

She wasn't sure what about the woman rubbed her the wrong way. On the surface, it seemed like she was just trying to be nice. But Diana couldn't help feeling that the second her back was turned, Marie would find a knife to drive into it. Maybe she'd take the necklace and head off with it. Grabbing her skirts, she hurried inside, still scanning the opulent palace for any sign of her lost jewels.

By the time she reached the grand main foyer of Versailles, the situation was all but hopeless. A depression settled over her as she stepped toward the doors and looked up at the sparkling chandeliers that until this day, she'd only seen in pictures. She'd waited so long for this and not only had nothing turned out like she wanted . . .

Now she was fairly sure she was in some pretty deep trouble.

Well, you have certainly gone and made this night an unforgettable one. Talk about a *Sliding Doors* moment. Maybe her decision to travel to Versailles for a night of decadent fun would lead her to spend the next twenty years in a French prison.

She imagined herself shackled to a wall in some Bastille-like prison cell with leaky walls and cockroaches, and her corset felt even tighter. Or maybe her fate would be more like Jean Valjean's in *Les Mis,* doomed to a prison and hard work for eternity. And he'd only stolen bread, not some priceless treasure. Did they have the firing squad here?

Shaking off those thoughts, she went outside to the tent where she'd rented her outfit. As she did, she sighed. She'd dreamt about this night forever. The party was supposed to go on all night, with fireworks and dancing until morning. But now, all she wanted to do was escape as quickly as possible.

Maybe Lily and Bea were right. Maybe I should forget the rest of the trip and just go home.

But with the lieutenant's words ringing in her head, she realized she couldn't even do that.

Sighing, she passed through the tent. The woman who'd helped her get ready, Colette, was gone now. The tent was almost empty with a small group of ladies sitting in folding chairs among the racks of gowns, sharing a bottle of champagne. One of them, the young willowy blonde with the stick-straight hair, stood up, "Hello, may I help you?"

She nodded, "I'm done." She started pawing at her dress out of frustration. "I'd like to get this thing off."

"Oh, but, mademoiselle, surely you are not done enjoying the party just yet? It goes all night! Don't you want to—"

"I am done. Please, show me where I can get changed."

The woman's accommodating smile fell from her lips. "I see. Right this way." As she led her down the aisle of empty dressing rooms, she said, "I am sorry if you did not have a good time."

Diana suddenly felt tears at the corners of her eyes. When had she ever cried in public before? She certainly wasn't going to do it now. She blinked them back, handed the woman the key to the locker with her belongings, and said, "I had a fine time. I'm just tired."

She stepped into the dressing room and slipped out of the dress, trying not to think of how excited, how *happy* she'd been when she'd put on the dress, not three hours earlier. She'd had a feeling that anything could happen, that her night was full of possibilities.

Well, anything *had* happened. And those possibilities had been *bad* ones.

When she pulled on her pants and her sweater, she looked at the beautiful dress, puddled in the corner. Just a short time ago, a dashing

Frenchman had recognized her, asked to dance. And she'd waltzed across the ballroom gazing deep into his eyes, thinking, *Maybe. Maybe tonight is the night when everything I dreamt of comes true.*

At that moment, a sob did force its way out of her throat, but she swallowed it down and patted her chest, pretending it was a hiccup. Then, inexplicably, she started to laugh.

Well, you sure made this night unforgettable. You are never, ever going to forget this day, that's for sure.

She pulled away the curtain and found the woman waiting for her with her folio. Diana reached into the purse and laid out the earrings and the fan she'd used along with the corset and gown and shoes. The woman went over it carefully. "I do hope you'll come again next year," the woman murmured as she scanned the receipt and marked checks next to each item.

Probably not, she thought to herself, holding her breath as waited for the obvious question.

Finally, the woman looked up, "It says here you had a necklace. The *Madame Royale* diamond. Beautiful diamond, that, worn by the lovely Marie-Thérèse Charlotte of France, Marie Antoinette's eldest child."

It was? The concierge had said something about that, but only now, did the full weight of it hit her. The necklace wasn't just valuable—it was priceless. Now, Diana felt even more terrible. "Yes, well—"

"That is a grand piece of history, I must say. She was given it as a present from her father Louis XVI on her fifteenth birthday, and it was the only treasure she was allowed to keep when she was forced into prison at the Reign of Terror. Some say she smuggled it in. Before she died in Slovenia in 1851, she announced that the diamond should never be parted from Versailles and donated it back to the palace for us to keep safe and for France, her homeland, to enjoy."

Okay. And I didn't think I could feel any worse than I already do. "I'm surprised it was rented out to be worn, considering how valuable it was."

"Yes . . . that is odd. We usually display it, but I've never seen anyone wear it."

Until me. So this great piece of French history ends with the silly American. What a great story. So . . . fantastic.

Gritting her teeth, she decided to get it over with: "I seem to have misplaced it. I was hoping . . . did no one turn it in here?"

The woman's eyes widened, and she let out a little gasp, "Misplaced? You mean, you lost it?"

Diana cringed as she nodded. *Misplaced* sounded a lot nicer, but tomato, tomahto. "Can you check to see if someone might have turned it in?"

The clerk stammered for a moment before saying, "*Oui* . . . Could you please wait right here?"

The young woman scurried to an older woman in the corner, and then the whispering started. Diana felt like she was in high school, being gossiped about by the cool kids as they both whispered and stared, whispered and stared. Then the older woman gasped and shook her head. Finally, the younger woman scurried off, and the older woman, with a mane of shiny silver hair to match her thick jewelry, appraised Diana, her face still a mask of utter shock and dismay. "My colleague just told me that you lost the Madame Royale?"

Diana sighed, "Well . . . yes. I simply can't find it anywhere. It must've fallen from my neck during the night. I'm assuming that it wasn't turned in by anyone?"

"No. Unfortunately not," the woman said, shaking her head ruefully. "We do have security, but, oh. It's a bit lax tonight. This is terrible. It's a priceless treasure. Worth millions. How could you possibly lose it? Weren't you taking care?"

The woman wasn't exactly doing a good job of making Diana feel better about this. In fact, the way she kept looking at her, eyes narrowed in something like disgust, Diana couldn't shake the feeling that she was being regarded as a criminal.

"I was taking care. And I never left the palace. So if I'd planned to steal it, it would still be on me. You can search. I don't have it. So it's probably still he—"

"No. That's not necessary." The woman glanced at Diana's purse, and Diana got the distinct impression that she was disappointed in her. Wary. "But I will have to summon security to look into this. They will probably want to search you, extensively."

Diana's stomach roiled. *My first trip to Versailles, my first body cavity search. Wonderful.* "Of course. Do you know . . . was it insured?" she asked carefully. "What I mean is, how does this work? Am I going to be on the hook for the whole cost?"

The woman just glared at her with an expression that said, *As well you should be, you careless fool.* Diana felt about two inches tall.

100

A moment later, the young woman returned with . . . perfect. Inspector Clouseau. Diana and he had remarkably similar reactions to seeing one another: they both rolled their eyes as if to say, *You again?*

He strode over to her and said, "Madame St. James. Are you the one with the missing necklace?"

"That's right."

He motioned to the police officer beside him. "All right, I want you to track Mme St. James' movements from the moment she left the tent with her. Map out every single step. Let's pull the security footage for those locations," he said. "No one is coming in or going out until we've found that necklace."

"You really think if someone took it, they'd hang around here?" she asked, incredulous.

He didn't answer. He was busy staring at her purse.

She handed it over. He took it from her and opened it, glanced inside, and gave it back.

"You've had an eventful evening, now, haven't you?" he asked with a condescending lilt in his voice. "You should head on back to your hotel, now. Get some rest. But don't go too far. We'll be in touch tomorrow."

She opened her mouth to speak but then caught sight of *them*. All of them. A little circle had gathered around—police, clerks who worked in the tent, a few straggling ball guests.

She was used to being in large groups, commanding attention. But usually, the people in her meetings regarded her with respect. With appreciation. The looks on these faces was so different, all Diana wanted to do now was melt into the scenery and disappear. They regarded her with close-lipped frowns. They averted their eyes from her whenever she looked directly at them. It was like they believed there was something wrong with her.

Like they believed she was *guilty*.

And she knew, right then, that if she wanted to change their minds, she was going to have to do something about it.

CHAPTER SEVENTEEN

The following morning, Diana rolled over in bed and stared at the ceiling. *What an unforgettable evening, Diana. Really, way to start this trip off with a bang.*

Though without the corset she could finally breathe freely, she felt like there was an elephant sitting on her chest.

The necklace. One-point-four million dollars of necklace, and according to what the police had told her last night, because she'd lost it, she was on the hook for every last cent of it.

Back in New York, when Macey had gushed about how fun her little jaunt abroad was, she'd neglected to mention things like this. She'd probably never had to deal with such things. The most she'd had to endure was a missed train to Lisbon. She probably hadn't had a single murder or theft on her trip. But Diana had had both—in one night. Some girls had all the luck.

Diana grabbed the remote and turned on the television. She flipped through the offerings, mostly cheesy Lifetime movies and Nickelodeon cartoons, all dubbed in French, until she came to the news. Sure enough, Versailles was featured front-and-center, the lead story of the morning. She saw the beautiful gardens she'd been walking through, and then a man began to speak in French. With some difficulty, she translated: "Murder and intrigue at the Versailles yearly costume ball, which is held on the summer solstice every year. It appears a man fell to his death from a balcony, and the priceless Madame Royale diamond, worn by Marie Antoinette's daughter, is missing. It is not known whether foul play is suspected. Police have not named any suspects and investigations are ongoing."

Diana winced as a picture of the gorgeous necklace appeared on the screen.

How could she have lost that? Was there foul play? She still didn't know, but if there wasn't, that was a big coincidence. All she knew was that they'd asked her about a million questions last night, most of them on repeat, and the whole time they mapped out her movements, they regarded her like the top suspect in both crimes. By the time she'd gotten back to the hotel, it'd been well after one in the morning, and she'd fallen into bed dead asleep almost the second she walked through the door.

She flipped through to another news channel, where she saw the familiar face of Inspector Clouseau. His real name, of course, *Lieutenant Pierre Bayans,* was on the bottom of the screen in a red ticker as he said, in French, "Yes, we were brought to the scene at just after nine in the evening after receiving reports of a dead man on the grounds of Versailles. He unfortunately fell from a balcony some twenty feet above the stone patio, and we're looking into whether this was intentional and interviewing possible witnesses. We are also investigating the strong possibility that the death of this individual is connected to the disappearance of the necklace."

Diana shivered. *Strong possibility.* There was nothing, really, that connected the two suspicious activities at all.

Nothing, that is, except her.

That thought tangled her stomach, making it rumble. She realized she was probably just hungry since she hadn't eaten anything from that sumptuous buffet at Versailles, so she picked up her phone and grabbed the room service menu.

She wanted to order one of everything, since she was feeling that miserable, but instead, when the attendant answered, she said, "Yes, can I please have a large carafe of coffee, and I don't know . . . do you have crepes?"

"For breakfast? Never! I'm sorry, Mme St. James, but crepes are not on our breakfast menu. We offer them for lunch and dinner—as a dessert."

She sighed. Now that she knew she couldn't have them, she wanted them more than ever. "Is there any way to bend the rules a bit, maybe?" She checked the clock. "It *is* almost eleven, after all?"

"Well . . ."

"I had a bit of a crazy night. Can you just see?" she added, sniffling a little, and immediately regretted it. It was undignified.

But, then again, so was traipsing around Versailles playing princess in a diamond necklace you had no business wearing.

"If not, I'll just take some croissants. Thanks."

"I will see what I can do, Mme St. James. Apple caramel or chocolate cherry?"

"Chocolate cherry, please. Extra whipped cream, if it comes with that. Just extra everything. Thank you."

She ended the call, climbed out of bed, and went to the window. Drawing back the shades, she could just see that sliver of the Eiffel Tower. Even now, it brought a little thrill of excitement to her. Though she'd already made herself a suspect in a crime, she was *here*. In the most romantic city on Earth.

And yes, anything could happen.

But that thought made her shiver. Anything *bad* could happen. So far, that was most of what she'd gotten. What if, like the woman on the plane, this year was the start of only bad things? What if no matter how hard she tried to live for the moment and make things amazing, it always fell short?

Or in this case, more than short . . . last night hadn't even landed anywhere *close* to amazing. It was, like, not even in the same time zone.

She went out onto the balcony and looked out over the railing, holding tight to the rail to rein in the dizziness she felt. Funny, she'd never felt vertigo before, but maybe it was something about seeing Luc's body, broken and twisted on the ground, that had forever scarred her.

She recalled the news story. The police were investigating foul play. *Had* someone pushed him? If so, who? She certainly hadn't seen anyone, had she? But if someone had . . . had that person anything to do with the missing necklace?

Possibly. But the only people she remembered were those drunken people who'd nearly knocked her down as they went past. The two women who'd come into the bathroom too. Them, and Luc. There was no one else that had even gotten close to her—except that fake Marie Antoinette and Inspector Clouseau, but that was after the murder. Even then, everyone seemed to be in a happy, partying mood. No one looked the least bit shifty, like they were about to steal a priceless treasure.

It made absolutely no sense.

Below her, a car honked, distracting her from the thought. She had a full day of sightseeing planned, but she'd already blown that out of the water, moping. Not to mention, she didn't really feel like going anywhere anymore. Her ribs still ached from the corset, and her feet hurt from the shoes. All she wanted to do was eat her crepes and crawl under the covers. Her nose was stuffy too. She was probably getting a cold.

A cool summer breeze off the Seine made her feel even more shivery, so she went inside and slid the balcony door closed. As she did, someone knocked on the door and called, "Room service!"

She ran across the room, opened the door, and let the man wheel the cart in, setting it up across from the television set. It was a lovely presentation—a silver carafe of coffee, dainty fine china and crystal goblets, and a little bud vase with a rose inside. She signed the folio and thanked him.

Then she slid into the chair and pulled off the lid over her breakfast. The scent of warm cherries wafted through the air, and she took in the lovely sight of the delicate crepes, covered in chocolate ganache, powdered sugar, and whipped cream. Someone had put the whipped cream in the shape of a smiley face.

It made her smile back.

But then she looked up at the news, and the smile fell away. They were back to another news story about the incident at Versailles. It was as if nothing else had happened in Paris but this murder. She was about to turn off the television when the picture of a handsome man in a modern tuxedo appeared.

It was Luc.

The reporter said, "The victim was identified as Claude Lachance, a history professor at a local college, whose wife was clearly distraught by the news of his death. She said that they had bought the tickets to the event months ago and had been planning to attend it almost since it was announced."

The screen flashed to a pretty young blonde woman who looked about twenty years younger than Diana. Who looked almost *exactly* like Vidal, the model Evan had traded her in for. The woman was sitting in her living room on a brocade sofa with a white cat in her lap in what appeared to be a very nice, well-appointed house, tears running down her cheeks as she recounted the tragedy of her loss. *"Je suis dévasté,"* she sobbed as her name, Veronique Lachance, appeared on the bottom of the screen. *I am devastated.*

Diana stared at the screen long after the report ended.

What. In. The. World?

She blinked, sure she was hearing things. Seeing things. That woman couldn't have been . . .

His wife?

No, obviously not. Something was wrong here. Where had she been at Versailles while Diana and her husband were tripping the light fantastic? The man she'd danced with had said he was alone in a forlorn way that had made Diana change the subject quickly, wondering if his wife had died.

Diana stared at the poor woman. Strangely, she felt *bad* for the woman. At least Evan had had the good sense to file for divorce from Diana before finding Vidal. And Evan wasn't a lowdown liar who made up names so he could pick up women.

Here this woman was, crying hysterically on national television over the husband she'd lost. The man she loved. The man she'd trusted with her heart.

The man who was clearly a piece of absolute scum.

Letting out a "gah" of frustration, she jabbed the button on the remote control to turn the television off, and almost threw the control across the room.

Claude Lachance? A history professor? What the heck happened to Lucien Beauchamp, cómte de Monteil de Saint-Quentin?

Here, she thought that as a New Yorker and no spring chicken, she was savvier than most.

But there was no question about it. She'd been had.

Of course, she'd been. Alone, in a strange city, feeling down about her lack of relationship status and ridiculously hopeful about rekindling some fairytale fantasy . . . what had she expected would happen? Lily had said as much. No, he was not an axe-murderer, but he was close. She'd had her one chance with Stéphane, and now fate was laughing at her, telling her that when it threw you good things, it was best not to throw them back.

Her dreams were circling the drain, ready to drop.

And maybe it was time to let them. To give up and go . . .

Home? She didn't have a home. She didn't have anything, really, to go back to. Not that she could anymore, anyway, with Inspector Clouseau breathing down her neck.

And since when did she give up? Never. She was the one who'd clawed her way up the corporate ladder at Addict. She was the one who'd earned the respect in that boardroom, not by giving up, but by showing them she knew her stuff, throwing her heart and soul into the business every single day, and facing hurdles head-on instead of running away from them.

So one thing was sure: if she wanted to salvage this trip—to turn it into the best year of her life instead of a raging dumpster fire—she needed to act.

She needed to stop sitting around, stuffing her face with crepes, and to get out there . . . and figure out what happened that night.

She studied the television screen, thinking of that poor unsuspecting wife. Then she took a giant bite of cherry-chocolate crepe and chewed without even taking the time to savor the flavor.

She was a woman on a mission now.

And Veronique Lachance was where Diana needed to start if she wanted to clear her name.

CHAPTER EIGHTEEN

Interestingly enough, when Diana popped Claude Lachance into Google, she came up with only one address, a flat somewhere in the fifth *arrondissement* near the Sorbonne, where she decided he likely taught. When she looked further, she discovered that yes, that was where he did teach. History.

Of course. That's why he knew all the stuff about Versailles, she thought as she shifted in the back of the cab on the way to the apartment. Maybe that was what he'd been doing—playing a part. She'd been too. They'd all been. That was why they'd been wearing costumes, after all.

But what on earth had happened to him after she left him?

It seemed hardly logical that he'd have fallen, she decided as she watched the streets of Paris pass by. The railing was a high, thick one, so he'd probably have only fallen if he'd climbed over for some reason. And he wasn't drunk. Murder made more sense.

Murder. She shivered at the thought. For what reason? Why kill a professor? Or was there some shady business he was involved in?

Well, shady business *other* than pretending to be a count and hitting on women who weren't his wife?

He *couldn't* have taken the diamond, she decided as the taxi turned a corner and Notre Dame came into view, the gargoyles poised on the pedestals everywhere staring down at her, mocking her. She'd had the necklace on when she'd left him on the dance floor, and the next time she saw him, he was dead.

But maybe he'd been hoping to lure her out there—to charm it from her. Who knew? Maybe it was a conspiracy. Maybe the man who'd given it to her to wear was involved too.

The cab pulled up to the curb, and she swiped her card. "*Merci beaucoup,*" she said, stepping out and looking at the row of modest flats. Not nearly as nice as the stately homes in the neighborhood Stéphane had called home but pleasant and well-kept. There wasn't a bit of garbage on the street or a broken window anywhere.

108

As she moved out of the shade of a willow tree planted at the curb, she checked up and down the street, half-expecting to see Inspector Clouseau with his magnifying glass raised to his eye surveying her every move. But the only thing she saw was an old woman, walking a teacup poodle down the sidewalk, and a couple of delivery men, struggling with a piano, a few doors down.

She checked the numbers, found the house that belonged to the Lachances, climbed the stout stone staircase, and rang the doorbell.

She saw movement inside beyond the gauzy curtains and, as she took a deep breath, readying herself to speak, realized she hadn't thought of a story. *Hi, I danced with your husband last night before he was murdered. Oh, and he invited me for a little tete-a-tete on the balcony, a little rendezvous, if you will. But don't worry, he died before we could do anything that would jeopardize your marriage vows.*

No, that probably wouldn't go over too well.

But the door had already swung open and standing there was the same woman Diana had seen on the television. Though there were no tears in her eyes, they were bloodshot, her face ruddy. She blinked, a little confused, and her voice was barely audible. "*Oui?*"

A number of possible lead-ins had crashed into Diana's head in the moments before the woman spoke. *I can be her husband's insurance broken? Collecting for charity? Home inspector? Selling magazine subscriptions? My car broke down, and I wondered if I could borrow your phone?*

Nothing seemed to work, so she finally blurted, "Veronique?"

The woman nodded. She was wearing a big shapeless cardigan over a daintily flowered silky sundress, squeezing it closed at the throat in a slightly defensive posture. "*Oui. Vous désirez?*"

Diana nearly choked. If she was going to pretend to be any of those things, she'd need more than the two years of conversational French she'd had in high school and the romantic phrases that Stéphane had uttered to her once a thousand years ago—that were now so embarrassingly etched in her head.

"*Bonjour,*" Diana started aimlessly. "I was wondering—do you happen to speak Eng—"

"Who are you? Are you American? Are you from the press?"

"No, of course not," she quickly clarified, fumbling for an excuse. What she was looking for was the best answer so that the woman might invite her in for a cup of tea. But nothing really presented itself. "I've just—"

"Yes?" Her eyes narrowed. She was annoyed now.

She looked over to her right and noticed the *A LOUER* sign in the window of the next flat. *FOR RENT.* In that split second, Diana decided to go for it. "I was looking to rent in the neighborhood, and no one answered next door. So I thought I would ask my potential neighbors what they thought of—"

"I don't know. It's fine. We've only lived here a year, but . . ." she shook her head and started to close the door. "*Excusez-moi,* but I am probably not the best person to ask, so—"

Diana nearly lunged forward to stop the door from shutting on her. "Oh, but I mean, is it close to public transport—"

The woman's eyes narrowed further. She spat, "You're one of them, aren't you?"

"I'm sorry, what?" Whatever the *them* was, it clearly wasn't anything good.

"One of his women."

She blinked. "I'm sorry?"

"Claude. His women." She eyed Diana up and down, "Usually, he goes for younger ones, his students, but . . ."

"You mean, you know about that?"

She laughed bitterly. "Of course, I do. I may look young, but I'm not an idiot. I'm the reason he divorced his first wife. I used to be a student in his class."

"Oh. So at the ball . . ."

"I didn't go to the ball. We bought those tickets a long time ago. But we've been in the process of separating for three months now. He doesn't even live here anymore, but every once in a while, a woman will show up on my doorstep—like you." She shrugged, "I didn't know what he was doing. I don't care to know, and honestly, it makes no difference to me now or even before his death."

Diana blinked. "But on the news, you seemed very upset . . ."

"I was surprised, yes. They woke me up in the middle of the night and told me, and it did shock me. They told me they think it's murder. Claude was a fool, but a lovable fool. He didn't have enemies." She shuddered, "I can't believe anyone would do that to him. It seems like a dream, like I'll wake up tomorrow and find out it isn't real. I can't believe he's gone."

Diana nodded. Having once fallen for a "lovable fool" herself, she understood. As much as she told people that she didn't care what Evan was up to, if she'd found out something that terrible about him, she'd be shocked too. "I met him at the ball," she said quietly, deciding to come clean. "The police say I might be the last person to see him alive."

"You were? What was he . . . was he acting strange?"

Diana shook her head. *Other than trying to charm me when he already had a wife at home, no.* "He seemed very pleasant. If he was worrying about something, one wouldn't know it by looking at him. And I'm a curious person. I was just trying to . . ."

"You were trying to see if I could give you any clues to what happened?" Veronique shook her head. "I'm sorry. I can't. I wish I could. I don't care how bad things were between me and Claude. Yes, he was dishonest. Yes, he was involved with things I didn't agree with and didn't care to know about. But he took care of me in the best way he knew how. If it's murder, I want to find the person who did it. He didn't deserve that."

"Thank you," Diana said, not sure if *I'm sorry for your loss* was appropriate considering they obviously weren't on the best of terms. She clearly needed to move on too. Diana decided not to bother her anymore. "I appreciate your time."

She went to step back, and the woman almost finished closing the door, but then she opened it wider. "I told this to the police, but it seems the media is coming up with all this wild speculation. Whatever happened, I'm sure it was an accident. That's all it could be."

She closed the door, and Diana climbed down the rest of the steps, thinking. If it was an accident, that meant the murder and the stolen necklace had nothing to do with one another. And that seemed like too big a coincidence to her.

Claude's wife may have been a dead end. But there were thousands of other people at the ball. Other people who had seen the necklace. And somewhere, out there, Diana was sure someone had seen something.

She just had to find that person and get them to talk.

As she was meandering down the street, her phone rang. It was a strange number. She picked it up, "Hello?"

"Hello, Mademoiselle. Bayans here. I called the hotel, and they said you'd gone out. I hope not far?"

Diana's stomach dropped.

CHAPTER NINETEEN

"No, of course, not far," Diana said. "Just out to do some sightseeing. I'm not in prison, am I?" *Not yet, at least.*

"Of course not. But I need you to stay close. We did have another question for you."

"All right. Fire away."

"A few people on the balcony mentioned seeing the victim acting rather strange before his death. Pacing and seeming rather agitated. Did you notice anything of the sort?"

"No." As far as she was concerned, he was smooth as butter. A charming rake, who used and disposed of women like they were tissues. "I didn't notice that at all."

"Did you talk of anything interesting?"

"No. He told me about the history of the palace. That was all."

"Did he mention your necklace at all?"

"No. I don't think so."

"All right. There will be more questions. Stand by."

And he hung up abruptly, leaving her clutching the phone to her ear, listening to dead air. Were they treating her with so little respect because she was American, because they thought she was a criminal, or both?

It didn't matter. She didn't like it one bit.

Since the weather was warm and sunny, the birds singing above, the sky the blue of a Caribbean Sea, Diana decided to walk back to the hotel and decompress. On the way, she passed Notre Dame, with its impressive flying buttresses, spires, and gothic architecture as well as the intricate stained-glass windows. *I am stopping by you, later,* she thought at it as she passed. *I promise. But right now, I have things to do.*

As she walked, again checking to see if anyone was following her, she thought about Luc. Claude. Why were there so many lovable foolish men in the world? It appeared America did not have a monopoly on them, which made Diana a little sad about her trip. She hadn't come on this trip to find romance, but in a way, it *had* been the impetus to get her here—that memory of Stéphane. So yes, part of her had thought . . . hoped . . .

Don't do that to yourself, Diana. You have far more important things to think about now.

Indeed, she did. She couldn't trust the police. If she didn't figure out what happened to that necklace, and soon, she'd *never* be able to leave France.

She'd noticed a display outside the restaurant at *Le Bonne Auberge* advertising a *coq au vin* lunch special, so she stopped in there and sat down at the bar, fishing for her itinerary in her purse as she went. She pulled it out, opened it up, and told the bartender she'd have the special and a glass of house wine.

As he went off, she buried her face in the book, grabbed a pen, and began crossing out all the things she'd missed, trying to arrange them for later. But her time was running short.

Besides, she had other thing on her mind. She'd meant to put in, somewhere, *Tour Notre Dame,* but instead put in, *Go back to Versailles?*

Tomorrow, she was due to leave Paris and take that drive toward the coast.

Sighing, she scratched all that out, too. It was *definitely* a good idea she hadn't booked those hotels everywhere like she'd planned to. Besides, maybe it would be easier just to take the train, instead of renting a car.

She flipped five days forward and saw the word *Florence* circled in black ink. She'd always wanted to visit Florence, almost as much as Paris.

If she didn't find that necklace, she'd probably have to cross Florence out too.

No, she told herself. *Paris may have turned sour. But over my dead body will I cross out Florence too.*

It was with that resolution in her head that her lunch came. She scooped up a little chicken in brown sauce and took a bite, savoring the taste. Perfect. All the food in France was always good

. . . was it possible for them to make a bad meal?

As she was wondering whether that held true for French prisons, someone slid onto the stool next to her. "Hullo, lass," a voice said. "Having a good time?"

She looked up to see her Irish friend, Sean from Ballygangargin. "Oh. Hi!" she said to him, rather surprised. She moved her journal over so he had room, and he ordered a pint. "How are you?"

"I'm fair. You're still writing in that little book of yours, planning things, I see?"

She nodded. "Making *changes* to plans, mostly. It turns out that I shouldn't have been so strict with my scheduling because things have been thrown off almost since the moment the plane touched down," she admitted.

He took his beer from the bartender and took a long gulp. "Aye, well, that'll happen, I'd say. Sometimes it's better to just go with the flow." He motioned to the bartender and indicated *I'll have what she's having.* "Now tell me, sweet lady, how was your soiree at the palace?"

She rolled her eyes to the ceiling, "An adventure."

"That so? You involved in any of the excitement all over the news?"

"Unfortunately. I spoke to the man. And I found his body."

She'd stunned him nearly speechless, "No kidding? You really found the man."

She shuddered at the memory. "Not to mention, I was wearing the necklace that was stolen."

He shook his head sympathetically, "Wow, you've been through the ringer, huh? Sorry to hear that. But from what I hear, you weren't the only one to have lost something there."

Diana had lifted her fork to take a bite but set it down. "What do you mean?"

"There's all sorts of news that a pickpocket was loose on the premises the day of the ball. After the excitement of the man's death, several people came forward and said they were also missing valuable things. It was in the papers."

"It was?"

"Yes! How does it feel to be a part of the Heist of the Century?"

He reached into the interior pocket of his corduroy jacket and pulled out a rolled copy of *Le Parisien*, which he unfurled on the bar. He pointed to the story, but Diana couldn't read well enough. She squinted at the words, trying to understand. "What does *la montre à bracelet* mean?" she asked, butchering the language.

He let out a short laugh and pointed to the heavy watch around his wrist. "Wristwatch. Apparently a very expensive gold watch was reported missing by one of the guests, and a few wallets. It's causing a pretty big stink and a PR nightmare." He shrugged, "I'll wager that might be the last Versailles ball for a long time."

"Oh," she said, but she wasn't really thinking about that. She was staring at the paper, trying to get more clues.

More things were missing. That meant that whoever had stolen her necklace had not just been targeting it. Likely, the person had gone after many things, brazenly. So shouldn't that have given police a better chance of apprehending the culprit, once the security footage was looked at?

Why hadn't the police made an arrest yet? What were they waiting for?

She stared at the paper, which showed a picture of a few police officers, flanking good ol' Inspector Clouseau as he gave a news conference. Off to the side, almost out of view, was the man in the ridiculous pink wig, who'd been at the jewelry counter and given Diana the necklace. She read down the article, where it featured a quote from him saying how terrible it was that this happened and how they'd never had such an event in all of his fifteen years of employment. His name was Blaise Chevrolet, and his title was Vice President of Concierge Services.

Diana tapped her fingernails on the bar, thinking.

"What are you up to, lass?" Sean asked, studying her closely, a hint of amusement on his face.

"Well . . . I was just thinking . . ."

"I'm sure you have a lot on your mind, considering how close you were to both crimes," he said, regarding her still with far more amusement than suspicion. "Do you think the two were connected?"

She shrugged, "I don't know. I get the feeling the police think they're connected because of me and that I'm the link."

"Did they say that you're a suspect?"

"Yes. Probably their main suspect. They've been calling me, and they wanted me to stay in the area. And I'm just worried that if they do focus too hard on me, they'll never find the real culprit."

"Ah. So that's why those little gears in your head are turning. You're thinking up a plan, aren't you?" he said with a smile. "I can tell. There is a sneaky look about you. You're up to no good."

"On the contrary, I *am* up to good," she said, picking up her fork and taking her second bite of the chicken. By now, it was cold, but still delicious. "I am going to make some inquiries and find out who did this. Starting right now."

CHAPTER TWENTY

That afternoon, Diana took the hotel shuttle back to the scene of the crime.

"Versailles?" the driver, who was different from the one who'd taken her there the night before, said when she told him where she wanted to go. "It is not a good time to tour there. The place is closed."

"Oh, I know," she said lightly, settling into the seat nearest the window and peering out at the Seine, sparkling in the distance. "I was there last night for the ball and misplaced something."

It wasn't a lie.

The driver, a large man with a goatee that wasn't quite helping to hide his many chins, glanced at her in the rearview mirror. "You see any of the excitement over there? It is all over the news."

By now, she didn't want to talk about it. It made her sick, thinking of draining her retirement account to pay for that necklace. "No. I just had a regular old time."

"What did you lose? Many things were stolen, they say . . ."

"Oh. Nothing valuable. Just a wrap." Okay, this time it was a lie. "Nothing a jewel thief would want."

"It was a shock, the Madame Royale disappearing like that," the man mused as he drove into traffic. "I saw it on display the last time I was there. You know, they auctioned off all of Marie Antoinette's jewels a few years back to private collectors. But that one, the palace kept. It was one of the nicest pieces, in my opinion. A symbol of France. I'd hate it to be gone."

Diana gritted her teeth. The last thing she wanted to do was be responsible for the destruction of a symbol of France. She might as well have sprayed graffiti all over the Eiffel Tower. "Hmm."

"So how long have you been in town, Madame?" the man said as she pulled out her itinerary.

"A few days."

He pointed over at the Louvre, unmistakable with its IM Pei pyramid sculpture out front. "Been to the museum yet?"

118

She looked over at it, a little wistfully. "No."

"What have you seen?"

Ordinarily, Diana would've been all for a little small talk. But right now, all she wanted to do was think about how she'd question the concierge. Likely, he'd be suspicious of her return, so she planned on using the whole "missing wrap" ruse on him. Somehow, she hoped he'd be able to give her a little insight into the other people who'd lost things. She wasn't quite sure how do go about that, though.

Not to mention that she hadn't seen much at all. Even at Versailles, she'd been too excited by all the fanfare and costumes and craziness that she hadn't really taken the time to enjoy any of the artwork or architecture.

Maybe she could do that now. That is, if they'd even let her in.

"Not very much," she admitted, burying her nose in the book. Luckily, the driver got the hint and let her be.

If she finished up here at Versailles by three, she decided she could maybe have the shuttle drop her off at the Louvre. They closed at five. Then, at least, she could say she'd done *something* on her itinerary.

The shuttle pulled through the honor gate that was outside the palace. As it did, she noticed the last remaining vestiges of the celebrations. Some workers in white coats were walking the gardens, picking up trash, and the disassembled tents and buffet tables were laid out on the lawn, waiting to be hauled away by the large delivery trucks parked along the curb. As the shuttle inched along the drive to the palace, avoiding the traffic, she leaned over and asked him, "Do you happen to know where the concierge office is?"

He shrugged. "I will drop you at the very front. There should be someone there who can give you directions."

"Thank you. Would you mind waiting? I shouldn't be very long."

He checked his watch. "I can only give you fifteen minutes. I have to pick up another party at the hotel and take them to the Bastille."

She checked her phone. "Okay. No problem. I shouldn't be that long. Just going to get my

. . . wrap."

"Good luck," he said, as she opened up the door and stepped outside.

The only problem was—just walking up the front pathway from the nearest drive to the individual guest entrance and through the arched doorway took a good five minutes. By the time she went through the massive double doors, she was already out of breath.

In the vestibule, she came to another set of doors. As she reached for one, it opened, and a man started waving her away, barking in clipped frantic French. He was wearing a suit and looking like he had done the same thing to countless other tourists over the course of the day.

"I'm sorry. I'm American. But I—"

"Okay, turn around. The Palace of Versailles is closed to visitors pending a police investigation. We will be open again soon. Thank you." He did a circle with his pointed finger, motioning for her to about-face.

"Actually, I was here last night? I left something here—my wrap— and was wondering if you had a lost and found," she said, clasping her hands together, ready to beg if necessary.

It wasn't. He tapped an earpiece on his ear, listened for a moment, and then said, "Yes. We do. All right then. Right this way."

He pushed open the door and let her go through the ticket check area, then began walking at a brisk pace toward one of the main hallways. As empty as it was, the foyer seemed even more vast and magnificent, but Diana didn't have a chance to take it in since the man was walking so quickly, his dress loafers clicking on the marble floor. Again, she was nearly out of breath by the time he stopped at a door that said, *pas d'admission sans affair. No admittance without business.*

He pushed it open and said, "Monsieur Chevrolet? This woman was at the party last night and says she misplaced her wrap. She'd like to look through the lost and found."

"By all means, send her in," a voice inside said.

He pushed open the door for her and let her pass into a room far too big and ornate to be just any office. It was the size of a tennis court with at least twenty-foot ceilings and had massive floor-to-ceiling windows and loud flowered wallpaper. The crown molding on the walls was detailed and exquisite. The only thing that made it obvious that it was an office, in fact, was the ornate mahogany desk at one corner, dwarfed by the sheer size of the room. That itself was somewhat of an antique with detailed carving and gilded accents.

To complete the picture, the man behind the desk should've been dressed in a waistcoat, stockings, and a powdered wig but instead was rather anachronistically attired in a modern black suit. After Diana's last trip to Versailles, his appearance there, signing whatever document in front of him with a ball-point pen, was slightly shocking and out of place.

He looked up at her over his bifocals. A smile came over his face, and he set his pen down. "Ah. *Mon cher mademoiselle!* So nice to see you again."

Diana squinted. For a moment, she thought him a stranger. But then she imagined him in a giant pink wig and powdered face, and it all came back to her. Right. It was Blaise Chevrolet, the man from concierge who'd insisted she wore the necklace.

"Hello," she said stiffly, unable to keep her emotions out of her voice. After all, if it weren't for his excellent salesmanship, she wouldn't be in nearly as much trouble as she was now.

He stood up and came around the desk. "What is this about you missing a little something?" He chuckled sardonically, "You misplaced something quite *significant*, but the police have that well in hand. There's nothing more you can do. In fact, I'd say you did enough already."

She frowned. *Yes, thanks to you.* "I misplaced my wrap."

"Did you?" He shook his head. "Unfortunately, with the police investigation going on, we really aren't allowed to have—"

"It's very important to me!" she blurted. "It's a . . . family heirloom. Belonged to my great aunt. And I'm leaving France in a few days, and I don't know what I'll do if I—"

He held up a hand like *Just stop already.* "Ah, well . . . I suppose. Just come along with me."

He tried to motion her out, but her eyes were too busy ping-ponging around the room. She wasn't sure what she was looking for. Something useful. She felt for sure that there were some answers in here.

He stepped out and cleared his throat. Reluctantly, she followed.

Back in the hallway, he motioned to the two brocade tufted chairs against the wall. "Have a seat, and I will see if I can retrieve the box of things we found after the party."

She sat. He started to leave, but she said, "From what I hear, a few people lost some things?"

He let out a disappointed sigh, "Yes. But that's normal for any party."

"I mean . . . like, expensive things. Like there may have been a pickpocket?"

He sighed. "Perhaps. The police are looking into it."

"Shouldn't it be easy with the security footage?"

"No. The fact is that during a party like this, security sometimes suffers. The rooms are crowded, and our cameras can't be everywhere. It's by far our largest and busiest event of the year, and people are drinking, having a good time. We have had our share of security concerns from time to time. Things go missing. However, nothing as prominent as the *Madame Royale.*"

"What sort of things went missing last night, Monsieur? I mean, in addition to the diamond necklace?"

He stared at her for a few beats as if unsure whether to disclose the information. "The usual things. A few wallets, a wristwatch. Just a moment."

As he headed off, his every movement seeming to echo through the giant building, she looked around. Every single piece of décor in the palace was probably museum-quality and worth a mint. Strange that the thief would've targeted the thing around her neck when he could've likely, very easily, lifted one of thousands of priceless valuables that were unattended during the party.

Then she looked up for security cameras. They were probably hidden because she didn't see any. Or maybe there were none to begin with. Maybe that was why the police hadn't come up with any answers yet.

She *needed* them. And the more she sat there, twiddling her thumbs, the more convinced she became that they were there in Blaise Chevrolet's office.

The second he disappeared from sight, rounding a bend at the far end of the hallway, she jumped to her feet and pushed open the door. She rushed to his desk, which was scattered with papers. Sure enough, there were a couple of reports there. Because they were written in French, she wasn't sure what they said at first. But then she spied the word, *la montre à bracelet.* Wristwatch.

"This is it," she murmured under her breath, her heart beating like crazy as she studied the name on the top line. Someone named Willy Laughler, who appeared to be staying at the Grand Paris Hotel, wherever that was. She kept repeating the name over and over to herself, committing it to memory, as she rifled through the rest of the papers. There were a few more too. The second one was for *Bronson Moreau, 62 Rue des Martyrs, 9.*

She said the addresses over and over to herself as she headed for the door and had just placed her hand on the doorknob when she heard a sound, outside.

It was the sound of Blaise Chevrolet's shoes, walking quickly down the hallway, toward her.

She backed up, behind the desk, trying to think quickly. Was there a window she could jump through? A trap door? Another exit? Yes, there was another door there, but it was all the way on the other side of the room. But the biggest thing in her head was, *This is a great way to take suspicion off you, Diana, rummaging through a man's private office.*

Outside, Chevrolet called, "Mademoiselle? Where have you gone?"

The pulse in her throat seemed to beat loudly in answer. She swallowed it back, hardly able to breathe.

The lock on the door clicked, and it slowly started to open.

Then she rushed behind the massive desk and ducked underneath, flattening herself into the thick oriental rug and wishing she could dissolve into it like a wine stain.

CHAPTER TWENTY ONE

This is really not how I expected my year abroad to begin.

That was the thought in Diana's head as she sprawled there, behind the desk, carpet fibers tickling her nose and making her think she had to sneeze. She wiggled her nose, trying to suppress.

Luckily, the desk was huge, allowing her to hide there, unnoticed. From her place on the floor, cheek pressed up against the plush oriental rug, she could easily see not only all the dust bunnies underneath the desk—there were quite a few—but Monsieur Chevrolet's shiny black wing tips as he hovered in the doorway.

He stepped inside, pausing tentatively there, likely wondering where she'd gone. The toes of his shoes faced toward the door, then pointed back into the room again, and then he started heading closer to the desk.

Closer to *her*.

She sucked in a breath and closed her eyes. Her heart beat so loudly she was sure Chevrolet would be able to hear its pounding.

Just then, the slight updraft of his movement sent one of the dust bunnies wafting over to her, coming to a rest right by her face.

The urge to sneeze became nearly overpowering. She exhaled heavily through her nose, trying to thwart the tickle.

Standing directly on the other side of the desk, Chevrolet let out a little grunt and muttered something in French that she couldn't understand. She heard him slide something heavy onto the surface of the desk. The lost and found box, she presumed. Then, she heard him picking up the phone, the slight beeping noise as he depressed the buttons. He spoke in rapid-fire French, sounding far less accommodating than he had been with her. She made out the gist of what he was saying: "Where is the woman that you escorted in here a moment ago?"

He paused for a response, which Diana imagined must've gone something like "No clue. I left her with you."

Then Chevrolet said, "Well, keep an eye out for her." Another pause, and then, "Hold on. I'll be right there."

He slammed the phone on its cradle and headed away. She watched as his black wing tips disappeared through the doorway and let out a sigh of relief as the sound of his footsteps faded.

Scuttling to her feet and smoothing down her skirt and blouse, she made for the door. She paused at the closed door for a moment, listening, and hearing nothing, squeezed out.

She'd only made it a few steps, her breathing on its way to returning to normal, when a voice behind her called, *"Arrête!"*

Wincing at the sound, she stopped, turning slowly. *I'm done. He saw me coming out of his office. I am so going to jail.*

But it wasn't Chevrolet. It was a man in a dark blue security uniform. He came closer to her, eyeing her suspiciously, and asked, *"Qu'est-ce que tu fais ici?" What are you doing here?*

She smiled broadly. Now would be the perfect time to be the dumb American tourist. No problem. *Which actually, considering what I've been up to, isn't that far from the truth.* She tittered. "I am sorry. I don't speak French. I got a little lost and I—"

"American?" His eyes narrowed in distaste.

"Yes, I—"

He rolled his eyes, "You're not supposed to be here. They should've told you that out front." He reached for his radio. "How did you get in?"

She nodded, "Yes. I know. Thank you. I just came in to take a look through the lost and found, and while Monsieur Chevrolet was fetching it for me, I had to use the bathroom. But I got lost—this place is like a maze!—and—"

"You said Monsieur Chevrolet knows you're here?" he asked, settling his radio back at his hip.

At that moment, Diana looked up and saw a sign across the hallway, clear as day, with the word, *Toilettes.* She quickly averted her eyes from it and nodded vigorously. "Yes. He generously had gone to fetch the lost and found box for me, and I'd—"

"There you are!" a voice called from down the hallway.

It was Chevrolet, heading toward her, a none-too-pleased look on his face.

She gave him a wave, feeling dumb. "Oh, hello! There *you* are!"

His gaze shifted to the officer, and back to Diana. "I was looking for you."

"Funny. I was looking for *you*," she replied, her smile on the verge of cracking.

"I thought I told you to wait outside my office. What happened to you?"

She pointed to the restroom. "Sorry. Powdering my nose. I must've missed you?"

He followed her outstretched finger and nodded slowly. "Oh. Okay. That's right."

"Well, anyway, thanks so much for your hospitality," Diana said sweetly, stepping toward the exit. "But I guess I should be going . . ."

"Mme St. James?"

She cringed at the mention of her name. Plastering that fake smile back on her face, she turned, knowing the next question out of his mouth would probably blow her house of cards down. "Yes?"

He put his hand on the doorknob for his office. "Did you not want to check the lost and found for your wrap? I brought it for you to look through. It's in here. *Remember*? Your *family heirloom."*

She cringed. *He is definitely on to me.* "Oh! Yes." *That was really stupid, Diana.*

She followed him in lamely, desperately wishing she could just leave before she did something else to announce her guilt. She was sweating profusely as she picked through the items in the box. A gold foil mask, a single shoe, a lace coin purse, someone's hat. There was a lacy fabric thing that *could've* been a wrap, but she didn't want to chance it by taking it, pretending that it was hers, and finding out it wasn't one. Of course, she already knew none of it would belong to her, but she put up the act and pretended to be really disheartened when her search came up empty, sighing big.

"Oh, too bad, it's not here," she said after a minute. "I must've left it elsewhere. But thank you."

"Anytime," Chevrolet said, sitting back in his chair and studying her closely. Suspiciously.

"I guess I'll be going," she said, backing away as if he was a panther, getting ready to leap at her.

"Yes . . . I guess you will. But if you give me a description of it, I can keep an eye out."

There was still something about the tone in his voice that told Diana that he didn't believe a word she said. That he knew exactly what she'd been up to. That he'd maybe even seen her, lying on the floor beneath his desk, but was playing along for the sheer entertainment of watching her twist in the wind.

"Well . . . it was . . . black," she said awkwardly, recalling a wrap she'd once had in her wardrobe. Ugly thing, she'd only worn it once before donating it to Goodwill. "With gold in it. And a fringe?"

Why did I phrase that in the form of a question? What am I, on Jeopardy?

He leaned over his desk and scribbled something down. "And where are you staying?"

"*Le Bonne Auberge.*"

"All right, Mme St. James, we'll be sure to let you know if anything like that shows up," he said, lacing his fingers in front of him. "And you be sure to let *us* know if you find that necklace."

He smirked.

She didn't.

She practically ran out of there, barely stopping to wave at the man at the desk who'd let her in the front doors.

Of course, when she got to the front curb, the shuttle was gone. She could hardly blame the man. It'd been way longer than fifteen minutes after all.

But she wanted to get as far away from Versailles as possible, as quickly as possible. She needed to get to Bronson Moreau. Grabbing her phone, she jabbed a call into the hotel. As she looked back at the enormous building, past the many windows and columns, she couldn't help feeling like she was being watched.

*

Bronson Moreau, 62 Rue des Martyrs, 6.

She blurted that to the driver of the shuttle, who just looked at her. By then, it'd been marinating in her head for an hour, and she was happy to get it out.

"I did wait for you, you know," he explained as he pulled from the curb.

She smiled, "I'm sure you did. I realize I was a bit longer than fifteen minutes."

127

"*Oui,* you were," he said. "But if you're not going to be long at your next stop, I can wait. Right now, I don't have any other calls coming in."

"That would be great. Thank you."

By then, they were heading through rush hour traffic, and so the drive of only a few miles took just over an hour. Luckily, the driver didn't talk much, allowing Diana to think about how to approach this man. She certainly didn't want a replay of her interaction with Veronique Lachance, so she decided to stick to a story that was as close to the truth as possible.

The man's home was in a section of the city similar to Stéphane's old home; in fact, it was only around the corner. Oddly enough, it felt like a lifetime since she'd stood outside the wreckage of his home. Back then, her heart had panged with excitement, believing her dreams were about to come true. And now . . .

Everything was different. Bleaker.

Almost as if to confirm the fact, the house was a solid, gray stone edifice, imposing and lacking any charm, like a bank building. She climbed the steps, wondering if that was indicative of the man who owned it.

When she rang the doorbell, it was instantly opened by a young Asian woman in jeans. "*Oui?*"

"*Bonjour.* I, um . . . *Parlez vous anglaise?* Does Bronson Moreau live here?" she asked.

The woman nodded, "Yes, he does. But Monsieur Moreau just returned from work and is indisposed."

"Oh. Are you his . . ."

"Housekeeper," she said. "Are you selling something?"

"No. I just had a question for—"

"*Qu'est-ce?*" a voice boomed from the top of the stairs, behind her.

Stiffening, the housekeeper turned and, with her voice shaking, mumbled something about it being some American woman. Diana could sense the woman was definitely uncomfortable. So, Bronson Moreau was a jerk.

Diana braced herself as the door swung open wider and the man appeared. He was probably mid-forties, dressed in a three-piece suit, wearing glasses. He had longish dark hair, slicked back from his face, and gave off the oily Wolf of Wall Street vibe.

"What do you want?" he snapped, pointing at a small silver placard that said *pas de colporteur* in the door's sidelight. "We don't accept solicitations here."

"I'm not. I was at the ball last night and had something taken as well. I just had a few questions for ask you?"

His frown deepened, showing wrinkles on his face. At first, she'd thought him younger; but with the wrinkles and the gray hair she now noticed at his temples, he looked almost her age. "I'm too busy for—"

"Please. It'd only take a moment."

He paused for a moment, considering it, then pushed open the door. "All right, you have me intrigued. Come in."

He turned back to his housekeeper, who was standing at the ready behind him. He barked, "Draw my bath," at her, and she scurried up the stairs as he strode into a room that was full of built-in bookcases and uncomfortable-looking antique furniture. Despite it being the dead of summer and air conditioning whirring in the background, there was a fire roaring in the fireplace.

He motioned at her to sit on the sofa, while he sat in the wingback chair and started to fiddle with his pipe kit. "What's this all about, Mme . . .?

"St. James. Diana St. James."

"The ball, you said?"

She nodded, "Did you have a good time?"

He snorted. "Is it possible to have a good time at things like that?" His eyes went to the ceiling. "I normally stay far away from such a farce, but a lady friend begged me to go."

"You're single," she blurted, not realizing she'd said it aloud until his eyes flashed up from the pipe he was filling with tobacco.

The side of his mouth quirked up in amusement. "Yes, I am. Perpetually. Despite the notions women have about changing a man, I assure them it's not possible with me. I've worked too hard in my life to share my wealth."

Now, it was Diana's turn to snort. *Gee, what a lovely man.* "Understood. I wanted to ask you about your missing item."

He nodded, lifting the pipe to his mouth, and struck a match. He puffed, lighting it up, and extinguished the match. As he blew out the smoke, something Diana didn't mind because it reminded her of one of her grandfathers, he said, "Yes. My wallet. You say you lost something too?"

"Yes. I did. Was the police response to your missing item sufficient? Do you think they'll find it?"

He laughed, "What do you mean? They found it later that night. On the body of the dead man. It was returned to me the next morning."

Diana paused, her next question forgotten—"It was found already?"

He nodded.

"On the dead man? You mean, that Claude Lachance?"

He grumbled a yes, seeming annoyed that she didn't get it the first time.

Her jaw dropped, and her cheeks flushed. That was a definite curve ball. That meant that despite whatever Veronique said about him being a decent, lovable fool, he was also a criminal. A thief. And it also linked the thieving and the man's death together. But if they were linked, why didn't Claude have the necklace on him when he was found?

"What about the wristwatch? And the other—"

He shifted in his seat, crossed his leg over his knee. "Don't know." His lips stretched into an oily smile. "I have friends in pretty high places. The police commissioner's a dear friend of mine. They take good care of me."

"Oh, well—"

"Hey, wait," he said, wagging a finger at her. "I remember you. You were the lady in red. *Oui*. I do. You were the one who found the body, right? You were the one the police said was wearing the Madame Royale when it was stolen!"

His voice had been steadily rising, and Diana felt called out. She stood up. "Yes, that was me, but—"

"Diana St. James. Right. They think you killed the guy and took the necklace!" He seemed pleased with himself to have figured it out. "Yes, the police are going to want to talk to you again."

Her pulse thrummed. "What? Why?"

"Don't take it from me, because it's only second-hand information, but it did come straight from the top. That's the running story they're compiling. The two of you were in cahoots, trying to steal the necklace. You were seen dancing together, after all. He attempted to run away with it, leaving you to blame, and you were having none of it. So you killed him."

She rolled her eyes. "That's ridiculous. The police searched me. I didn't have anything!"

130

"Maybe. But I bet they think you hid it somewhere on the premises—to be recovered at a later date."

She clenched her teeth. That was wonderful. That meant, by going back to Versailles, she was looking guiltier than ever. "They may think that, but it's not true. I'm here now because I'm trying to find out who *did* steal the necklace."

He laughed. "According to the rumors, he's dead. And you're his accomplice."

"That's . . ." There were so many thoughts in her head, but every one of them died before they could reach her vocal cords. The last thing she needed was to implicate herself more. "I never met the man before that night."

He shrugged, "You might have to explain that to a judge."

She stood up, her pulse buzzing in her body, a fresh sweat breaking out on her forehead. She bolted for the door, hardly stopping to say goodbye. *No. I'm going to find that necklace before I have to.*

CHAPTER TWENTY TWO

So this is what it's like to be a wanted woman.

Diana looked up and down the street as she descended the stairs to the shuttle, where the driver was parked, waiting for her. There were no detectives dressed in raincoats, no hooded figures hiding in the shadows, tracing her every move, and waiting for her to do something wrong. At least, none that she could see.

Right now, she just wanted to get away from accusing eyes.

She quickly ducked into the shuttle and directed the driver to take her back to the inn. The sun was slipping behind the buildings and it was getting darker. Lights were popping on all around, and in the distance, she spied the Eiffel Tower, awash in a gleaming rainbow of color. Everywhere she turned, it was like it was screaming at her to come and be a part of it. Yes, the City of Lights was beautiful, and she should've wanted to enjoy it. But she had no interest in a nice dinner out in Paris. She just wanted to be alone in her room and think about her next steps.

As she was trying to catch her breath and stop herself from cringing over her latest missteps, her phone rang. It was Lily. She answered. "Hello, dear," she said tiredly.

"Mom! You sound tired."

"Well, I am."

"Too much exploring?"

She wished. She wished that she'd been gallivanting all over Paris seeing the sights, and now she was returning to the hotel for some rest. After all, that was the way this adventure was *supposed* to go. But she didn't want to go into it. "Yes."

"Mom? God! What's going on? First you go abroad and don't even bother to call me for days to tell me that you're okay, and then you give me one-word answers. Something's not right."

Diana sighed. "I'm not in the clutches of axe-murderers, if that's what you were thinking."

"Okay, well, then tell me! How was Notre Dame? The Eiffel Tower? The Louvre? And that ball? Was it everything you hoped it would be?"

The shuttle pulled up to the curb. She was already thinking of ordering a big glass of wine to take the edge off. Maybe two. Maybe a bottle. The last thing she wanted to do was recount the events of the past few days. And she wasn't even in the mood to make up little white lies about it. So she climbed out of the shuttle, waved at the driver, and mumbled, "It's fine, but I really have to—"

"Mom! I want details!"

Right. This was Lily she was talking to. Lily was always the one who needed to be in the know. Diana sighed, "All right. I'm just getting back to the hotel. If you give me a second,

I'll—"

But her voice died the second she passed through the revolving door. Her spine stiffened and her pulse quickened.

Standing in the middle of the lobby was Inspector Clouseau.

Hotel guests wove around him, giving him curious looks, and for good reason. He clearly wasn't your average tourist. The overcoat despite the warm weather and the suspicious way he was scrutinizing everything screamed—Man of Law.

Diana fought back the urge to take the revolving door all the way around and leave, deciding that if he caught her, it'd make her look even more suspicious. She paused there, watching him squinting at a map of the hotel, until he turned and noticed her. He stalked over to her. "I need a straight answer from you, Mme St. James. Why were you poking around where you shouldn't be?"

"What?" she asked, still holding the phone to her ear.

"Come with me," he demanded. "I'd like to ask you some more questions about the murder of Claude Lachance."

Diana glanced around. The hotel concierge was studying her, wide-eyed, as well as most of the people behind the check-in desk. A few guests in the lobby were also looking at her. She wasn't a fan of hard-boiled crime shows but she knew that when a detective wanted to bring a person in "for questioning," they often didn't see the light of day for a long time afterwards, if ever. "Are you arresting me?"

"Arresting you? Murder?" Lily's voice piped in. "Wait . . . did that guy just say murder? Who are you with?"

"No. I'm not bringing you in. I have questions." The lieutenant looked around. "Would you prefer to go somewhere more private?"

She nodded.

"Mom!" Lily screamed. "What's going on? Hello?"

"It's nothing, darling. I'm just catching the end of *CSI*. Can I call you back later?" she asked, pulling the phone from her ear to jab at the End Call button. Before she could, she heard Lily screaming about how she knew that wasn't the television because since when had Diana ever watched that stuff?

"Is that a code word, Mom? Are you in trouble?"

She probably should've answered and told her she was fine; but she was too flustered with the detective breathing down her neck; and by then, her finger was already on the red button, disconnecting the call. A second later, the phone rang again, from Lily, but Diana shoved it in her pocket. "Yes. Please."

She followed him down the hallway to a small card room with a large round table in the center. He was polite, pulling out the chair for her and waiting for her to sit; but the second he sat down, he launched into the attack. "Why were you at the deceased's home yesterday?"

Under the table, she dug her fingernails into her thighs. Her first impulse was to deny it, but then she lost her nerve. "I—" she stammered.

"The wife called the cops and said you were there," he said, pulling out a pad and flipping through it. "You spoke to Veronique Lachance. What did she say?"

Diana shrugged. "Well, if she called you, you should know."

"Did you know he was married?"

"No. I knew nothing about him. I just met him that night," she said. He studied her, clearly wanting more. She sighed. "And I went to his house, yes. Mostly because you were blaming me, and I knew he was a philanderer, and if he had no compunction about cheating on his wife, I thought there were some other shady things he might be involved in. I thought she could shed some light on who he was. Whether he had anything to do with the necklace."

"And?"

She shrugged. "I'm sure she told you the same thing. Nothing. She knew her husband was a cheat, but she didn't care to know anything else he was involved in. So it didn't get me anywhere."

He nodded, agreeing with her assessment.

"I was right, though. He was a thief. He stole a man's wallet."

Lieutenant Bayans' eyes flashed to her, full of surprise. "And how did you know that?"

She raised both palms to the sky, innocent. "I might have run into one of the other guests, who told me that his wallet was found on the body."

"How fortunate for you." He closed the pad. "But yes, that's true."

"And what about the wristwatch?"

Again, he looked surprised. "Now, Mme St. James, listen to me. I hope you are not trying to interfere in this investigation. Because if you do, you might find yourself in trouble. Big trouble."

If it was a threat, it wasn't spoken like one. His voice was like that of a big brother, looking out for a reckless child. She nodded. "I'm not. I know that. The last thing I want to do is interfere."

"Good." He pushed away from the table and stood up.

"Nevertheless . . . the wristwatch?"

His frown deepened, and he scratched at his moustache as his eyes went to the ceiling. At first, she thought he wasn't going to answer the question, but then he sighed. "The Rolex wasn't found on Lachance's body. In fact, all we found with him were a couple of wallets, which were returned to the owners. Happy?"

"Thank you," she said.

She wasn't happy. Now, she was more curious than ever. Did that mean there were two thieves at the ball?

After he left, she quickly grabbed her phone and googled the Grand Paris Hotel. Turned out, it was only a fifteen-minute walk away. And it was a beautiful night, too beautiful to be spent indoors when all of Paris was waiting for her, alive outside her doors. Besides, she felt like she was on the trail, making progress. And asking questions *wasn't* interfering. It was simple curiosity.

So the wine could wait. The answers couldn't.

CHAPTER TWENTY THREE

The Grand Paris Hotel was anything but grand.

It sounded as if it would be better than her little inn, but she'd nearly missed it when she followed her GPS along to a rather seedy area of town. She actually had to backtrack to find the front door, sandwiched between a Thai restaurant and an insurance agency. The sign above the door was so faded she could barely read it.

She went inside, looking around for the reception area among a sea of ferns and other indoor plants. The ceiling was low to begin with, and the many plants and dark-paneled walls gave the place the overwhelming feeling of being in a deep, dark jungle. She pushed aside the fronds as she pushed through and nearly tripped on a cat on the way to the reception desk.

A man with a Rolex was staying *here*?

At first, she was sure she had the wrong address; but when she found the old man sitting at the reception desk and asked, "Bonjour. Do you have a Willy Laughler staying here?" she was surprised when he nodded.

"Would you be able to call his room and tell him I'd like to speak with him?" she asked.

The old man's face pinched into a scowl. "Why. You a friend of his?"

"No. I'd just like to—

"You his mother?"

Mother? So he was younger? Or did she look that old? "No, I don't actually know him, and he doesn't know me, but I'd like to—"

"That boy is nothing but trouble to me. You police again?" Before she could answer, he said, "I do everything right. Take care of this place. Never bothered by the police. Then he comes to stay, and they're always here, bothering me. Americans."

"He's American?"

The man nodded and motioned vaguely, "I think he went next door to get food."

"Oh. Thank you."

She navigated her way through the minefield that was the lobby again, and went to the small place next door. When she stepped inside, the spicy scent of Thai food made her mouth water. It'd been a long time since her *coq au vin,* but she placed a hand over her rumbling stomach, trying to focus on the patrons. There was a tall kid with long, shaggy hair at the front of the line, next to a blonde girl who was substantially shorter than him. He looked nothing like the type of man who'd own a Rolex or go to a ball, but other than him, there was a woman with her kids, and a couple of women eating at the tables.

When he turned and started striding toward her, she took the chance and jumped in his way. "Mr. Laughler?"

He had a long, pointed nose and acne scars, wore a rumpled Rip Curl t-shirt, and wasn't particularly attractive in any way. His girlfriend, on the other hand, was beautiful and reminded Diana of Vidal. "Yeah?"

"Were you at the Versailles ball?" she asked him.

He nodded, "Yeah. Wait . . . you from the palace? You find my watch?"

"No, I'm not. I'm—"

"Hey, you're American?"

She nodded. "Yes, I was at the ball, too, and—"

"Hey!" He held out his fist. She knew what a fist bump was, but she'd never actually given one to someone. She did it, carefully. "We Americans got to stick together."

"Right. Well, I was at the ball too, and—"

"Yeah. Wild time. Really wild."

She couldn't be positive, but she thought she caught the scent of pot, mixing with the Thai food. She couldn't help it. She had to ask, "You enjoy going to events like that? A masquerade ball?"

He laughed, "No." He motioned to his girlfriend. "That was for the little lady. She actually won it on a radio call-in show, didn't you, Blossom?"

She nodded.

He beamed at her, "She's good at trivia. She actually answered a question about *Hamilton.* She loves that musical. She's nuts about it."

Diana smiled, feigning interest, "That's great. You won the whole trip?"

"Yeah. Whole thing. All expenses paid."

Interesting. Now, swinging it on back to the topic at hand . . . She couldn't find a good segue, and by now, she was tired and hungry, so she simply blurted, "I lost a necklace. And I wanted to know about how you lost your Rolex. That was yours, right?"

"Yeah, dude. Don't remind me. It was a gift from my parents, when I graduated high school. They thought if I had a watch . . . I'd ... I don't know . . . be responsible suddenly or something. Trade in my surfboard for a real job or something. Anyway," he laughed. "Didn't happen. The 'rents are gonna be buggin' when they find out I lost it."

"Lost it? Or had it stolen?"

A wide smile spread over his face, and he shrugged sheepishly, "All right. You got me. I don't know. Wasn't exactly coherent most of the night. Met a bunch of people, and we kind of went a little crazy." He looked over at the girl, "Right, Blossom?"

The girl gave an uninterested shrug and pulled a long string of gum out of her mouth.

"Anyway, that's why I didn't bother filing a report with the police. I think it's long gone. I spent most of the night puking in a fountain. It's probably in there, a home for fish or something. I told security at the ball, and they said they'd keep an eye out for it. But that's it. I don't think I'm getting it back. Man, my dad's gonna murder me."

Suddenly, Diana flashed back to that group of drunken young people who'd rushed out of the doors of the balcony, arms linked, knocking her to the ground. She vaguely remembered the blonde girl, hair done up in ringlets, and a tall guy, in the center of the fray. "I think I remember you," she said. "You were out on the balcony where that man was later found dead, right?"

His face fell. "We missed all the commotion about that. We were in the garden by then."

She replayed his words in her head, and another thing hit Diana. "Wait . . . you spoke to security. You didn't file a report with the police?"

He shook his head and started to speak, when something came over him. "That's a good point, dude. If I didn't tell anyone but security, how'd you know about it?"

She said, "Well, I—"

Blossom, who up until that moment had been as silent as one, suddenly piped up. "Hey. I remember her. She was on the balcony when that guy was killed."

138

Willy pushed the hair out of his eyes and squinted. "Yeah? You think so?"

"I know it! I wasn't as blasted as you were," Blossom said.

Diana backed away. People in the restaurant were beginning to stare. The man behind the counter with the giant chef's knife was particularly threatening. "I was, but—"

"Are you the one who lost that necklace? You are, aren't you?" Blossom said, her jaw dropped. "I remember you wearing it. I thought it was *boss*."

"Well, yes, but—" she stopped. "When you saw me, I was wearing it?"

She began to say something, but Willy spoke over her. "Don't talk to her, Blossom. There's something wrong with her. She probably killed that dude and is looking to put the blame on us. Let's get out of here."

He reached for the door, and she instinctively reached for his arm. "Wait, I—"

He stared at her arm, barely touching his bare elbow. His voice was low now, serious. "Don't. Or I'll call the police. My dad's a U.S. senator. He can *end* you, no problem, lady."

Willy and Blossom stepped out into the night, and Diana decided it was best not to follow. But that was interesting. She'd been wearing the necklace when she went onto the balcony. So that meant it had been stolen between that moment and the moment she realized it was missing, after she found Claude Lachance's body.

All sorts of bad things had happened that night on that balcony. Now that she knew the what and the where, she just needed to find out who and why.

CHAPTER TWENTY FOUR

Diana walked back toward the hotel, feeling a bit aimless, which wasn't really good considering it wasn't the best section of town. She kept looking over her shoulder, wondering if she was being followed. Eventually, she got past the Bastille and into a more touristy section of the city, where people were out, taking in the sights at night. She walked past a few couples walking arm in arm along the Seine; a couple of painters standing on the bridge in front of easels, capturing the cityscape under the bright lights; a man playing an accordion with a tiny pup and a cup for spare change at his toes. She tried to absorb all the energy of the City of Lights and enjoy the beauty around her. Instead, she couldn't stop thinking of that mysterious night at Versailles.

Claude Lachance, aka Luc, was a liar, a philanderer, and a thief. That much was clear. But she hadn't seen him on the balcony until she'd found him dead, and when she'd arrived on the balcony, she'd been wearing a necklace.

Diana didn't know a lot of things, but she was pretty sure dead men couldn't steal. So what had happened? When had it gone missing?

As she walked, her stomach rumbled, and she realized that it had been a good eight hours since her meal at the hotel. She stopped in front of a place with a sign that said *Café Saint-Germain* and, on a whim, stepped inside.

Despite the late hour, the place was packed. Definitely a good sign, and the smells wafting through the air promised good food. Though Diana's stomach was screaming for food, her head ached for a quiet place to sort out everything she'd learned. This wasn't it. She made out a note or two of piano music, but couldn't see the piano through the bodies waiting for a table, or make out the song because of the noise level. Her first thought was to turn around, but before she could, a woman at the hostess stand waved to her, "*Bonsoir!*"

"Hello," Diana said. "I just wanted a quick bite, but it looks like you're booked for the night."

She picked up a menu. "We don't have tables, but there is room for one at the bar?"

Diana nodded. The case could wait for an hour while she took care of her stomach. "That's fine."

The woman guided her through the throngs and packed tables to the edge of the bar. She sat down and opened the menu. Her stomach immediately pointed her to the salade niçoise, a perfect complement to a glass of sparkling white wine and a nice, light change of pace from the heavy coq au vin she'd consumed earlier.

When the bartender appeared in front of her with a flute of champagne, she wondered whether he was reading her mind. "Thank you . . ." she said, taking a sip. "I needed that."

He smiled at her and pointed toward the opposite end of the bar. "From the gentleman over there, at the end of the bar."

"Oh?" She blushed a little to find an older man, his bald spot shining in the overhead light. When he smiled at her, she noticed he was missing a couple of important teeth. He was well-dressed, at least, in a white shirt and tie.

Lily probably would've told her to go for it—what did she have to lose? But Diana was not in the mood to be charming. Not at all. In fact, she wasn't really in the mood to talk at all. It was too late to decline the drink, though, since she'd already taken a sip. So she asked, "Could you tell him I appreciate it, but I'm in a relationship?"

He nodded, "And what can I get you?"

"The salad. Thanks," she replied, digging out her phone. Of course, she had about forty missed calls and twelve messages from Lily, each getting significantly more frantic, and, later, similar messages from Bea, who Lily must've dragged into it. She quickly jabbed in, *Everything is fine! I'm tired. I'll call you tomorrow.*

She looked over to see the bartender speaking to the lothario on the other end of the bar. As he spoke, they kept looking over at her.

Diana quickly looked away as a message came back: *How do I know this is you? What is that stuff about murder? You HAVE to tell me!*

She sighed. *It's nothing. I promise. Everything is fine.*

She hated to sound like a broken record but she really didn't want to get into it with anyone. She just wanted to sit, relax, and enjoy her meal, without *any* outside distractions. Was that too much to ask? She reached for her glass of champagne and drained it so fast the bubbles tickled her nose. It made her think of the ball, and how she'd sipped champagne with Luc. Claude. Whatever. And what a nightmare that had been.

The next time she looked up at the bar, though, the lothario was no longer seated at his stool. What, had she disappointed him so much that he'd had to high-tail it out of there? She scanned the room and made out his bald head between the crush of people. To her horror, he was coming closer to her, his eyes trained on her like a leopard zeroing in on its prey.

Great. Doesn't take no for an answer. That's perfect. Helplessly, she looked up at the bartender, who shrugged and said, "Sorry. He seems to think he can change your mind."

Oh, no, she thought, looking around for an escape. Behind her was a doorway that led to the toilets. She jumped off her stool as quick as she could, grabbed her purse, and started to rush for it. She'd only managed two or three steps when a waiter stepped out of another doorway she hadn't seen, carrying a tray. In the last second, she skirted away to avoid him, finding herself pressed up against a booth, where a group of young men were talking in rapid-fire French. It was like she'd shown up to their conversation uninvited, because they all stopped and stared at her. She looked over her shoulder. The bald man had gotten to her spot at the bar and was now looking for her.

"Sorry," she said to the men. Whirling away, she'd just spotted a clear path to the bathroom and began to rush for it when someone stepped backwards. The toe of her shoe caught the other person's heel, and she went flying, falling flat to the ground and sliding slightly, putting her hands out at the last minute to stop her nose from smacking the grimy wood floor.

But the pain barely registered.

Instead, it'd sent her mind spiraling, thinking back to the last time she'd felt such embarrassment. She'd been wearing that red ballgown at Versailles, and those drunken people had gone by, and suddenly, she'd lost her balance and gone flying. And then . . .

Then that man had come by. He'd helped her up. He'd said, *Here, let me help you,* and lifted her to standing. *There you are. No harm done.*

As people rushed around her, trying to make sure she was all right, she realized that that man hadn't. He'd helped her up, but then he'd disappeared in a flash, not asking if she'd hurt herself or twisted anything. He'd left almost too readily.

She rolled over and sat there, ignoring the people asking if they could help her. Too readily. As if he was making a getaway. As if he had something to hide.

The necklace.

But what else could she remember about him? Nothing, except . . . the mask. The black mask with the gold accents. Likely, part of the huge costume department at Versailles.

She let out a shaky breath. Maybe she'd never know who killed Claude Lachance, but now, light was falling on the identity of the jewel thief. Yes, that could be it. That could *definitely* be it.

Diana jumped to her feet just as the bald man broke through the crowd and extended his hand to help her up. *"Bonsoir,"* he said to her, in what had to have been his deepest, most charming voice.

"Thanks for the drink," she said hurriedly, already pushing through the crowd. "Maybe we'll meet again. But right now, I have somewhere to be."

And without waiting for his response, she pushed her way out of the café and into the warm summer night.

CHAPTER TWENTY FIVE

Diana barely slept at all that night. Too many things were going through her mind.

Last night, she'd wanted to rush right over to Versailles and see if her suspicions were correct. Unfortunately, when she arrived at the hotel, the shuttle bus driver was off-duty, and then concierge told her that Versailles had closed at 8:30 p.m. Paris, unlike New York, was a city that slept. So she'd gone up to her room, ordered a salad via room service, and wolfed it down quickly as she plotted her answer-finding itinerary for the following day.

That was why, at precisely seven-thirty in the morning, she was dressed and downstairs in the lobby, ready to be the first stop on the shuttle driver's list. As she walked through the reception area, the concierge waved to her. "Mme St. James? A package arrived for you."

"Oh?" she asked, at first thinking that it might be a gift from someone. But as the concierge pulled out a flat envelope, Diana's spirits fell. Oh, right. The divorce papers from Evan. "Keep them there, for me, please? I'll get them later."

She rushed outside. When she got to the shuttle station, he wasn't there, so she kept checking her phone and tapping her foot until he arrived.

It was the same driver as the day before. She climbed into the shuttle, he looked back at her. "Let me guess. Versailles?"

"Oui," she said.

"I should warn you, it's not open for tours for another couple of hours . . . but I get the feeling that's not why you're going there."

She nodded distractedly, checking her itinerary for the day and scratching out just about everything on it for the morning. *Maybe,* if she was lucky, she could make it back in time to visit Notre Dame. "Yes, I need to speak to the concierge."

"Still looking for that wrap of yours?" he asked, scratching his fleshy chin as he pulled out from the curb into the early morning traffic.

"Yes. Something like that," she said, burying her nose in her phone.

He chuckled, "Well, I expect in a place as big as that, it could be anywhere."

She hadn't spoken to Lily since she'd been forced to hang up on her yesterday afternoon, so she quickly put in a call to her. Lily answered at once, "Thank God! What happened to you?"

"I told you I was fine. Just busy."

"Why was that man talking about a murder?"

"Oh, he was just using it as a figure of speech. It wasn't literal."

There was a pause. "I heard there was a murder at that ball you went to . . . a couple nights ago. Did you know anything about that?"

Diana blinked. So the news had gotten all the way over to America. Wonderful to be involved in an international scandal on her first week out of the country. "I heard about it, yes. Of course. Everyone did."

"You still haven't told me anything about what you've seen or done," Lily said with an accusing tone. "Am I going to have to read about it in the book? Or is this the way you're going to be for the year? Completely too busy to talk to the family that loves you?"

"Now, Lil—"

"I'm really doubting that you're even going to come back for baby, now. I bet by then we won't even know where you are!"

"I'm *definitely* coming back," she said immediately. "Of course, I'll drop everything. I promise."

"Okay," she said, the doubt still prevalent in her voice.

"How are you feeling?"

"Same as before. Just tired."

That makes two of us, Diana thought, yawning. She peered out the window just as the gates of Versailles appeared. "I'm heading off. I promise, I'll call you soon, and I'll fill you in on everything."

"Where are you going to now?"

"Oh, um—I'm hoping to get to Notre Dame." *Eventually.*

"Okay, Mom. I love you. Be safe."

"You too, love," she said, ending the call. The driver was watching her, now just as suspicious as everyone else. *Get in line, buddy.* Yes, she knew she was acting crazy. But really, if she could just find this mysterious man with the mask, maybe she could put an end to those questioning looks.

Not to mention, it'd *really* be nice to not be on the hook for the price of that necklace.

Versailles was much busier that morning because the place was finally opening. There were already tour buses and people milling about, lined up at the doors to buy tickets and taking in the gardens. Diana got out of the cab, went across the yard, and walked up to the ticket desk. "Admission for one?" the woman said in French.

Diana shook her head. "No, I am here because I'd like to talk to Monsieur Chevrolet?"

"Who?"

"Chevrolet," she repeated, louder. "The concierge? I lost something, and he was helping me find it."

"Ah. One moment," she said, then stepped away from the box. Meanwhile, behind her, someone in the line cleared his throat, obviously impatient.

She glared back at him. *Hold your horses,* she thought. *The museum isn't even open yet!*

A moment later, the clerk returned. "I'm sorry. Monsieur Chevrolet isn't in. You'll have to come back some other time."

Diana frowned. She needed to know the name of the man who'd rented that mask, and he was the only person with that information. "What is he, off today?"

She shrugged. "I don't know."

"You don't know? But when can I come back and speak with him?"

"You can call the office, later." She grabbed a brochure and slid it under the plexiglass divider. "Main number. Next, please."

Diana took the brochure, gazing with longing toward the doors to the palace. They were open now, and people were starting to filter in. People with tickets, at least. They were all getting closer to the answer than she—stuck outside in the vestibule—was.

The man behind Diana moved forward in the line, coming dangerously close to nudging her out of the way. She didn't budge. "Wait," she said, glaring at the man who'd invaded her personal space, like *back off.* She fumbled with her purse. "I'll take a ticket."

"Combination with the shuttle bus tour?"

She shook her head. "No. Just the—" she pointed ahead. "Just the palace."

The woman printed out the ticket. "That will be twenty euros."

Diana handed over her credit card, anxiously watching the crowds going in. Crowds were good. They'd certainly helped the pickpockets

146

at the ball to commit their crimes. Maybe they would help Diana to commit hers.

Not that it really was a crime. She was just going to *accidentally* get lost among the many rooms in the palace. Again. That was all.

The moment she got the ticket, she rushed forward through the doors. She handed the slip of paper to the ticket checker, who was dressed in period costume, much like she'd been at the ball. He studied it. "*Excusez-moi*, Madame," he said. "Your ticket is for nine. It is only eight-thirty."

She stared at it. Sure enough, that's what the ticket said. "Oh. Well, can't I . . . a little

early . . .?"

He shook his white-powdered wig head, "I'm sorry, that's impossible."

"But I . . . have to go to the bathroom?"

He frowned, "There are public restrooms located outside."

Again, someone behind her cleared his throat. She looked back and saw the same man, and grumbled, "He's not going to let you in. It's only eight-thirty."

The man, who clearly didn't speak English, simply glared back at her.

"What can I do?" she asked, lacing her fingers together in front of her, eyes pleading.

He motioned over her shoulder, "You can shop in the gift shop and get something to eat at the café while you wait."

Beaten, Diana hoisted her purse up on her shoulder and retreated to the crowded gift shop. People were packed in there, browsing the many aisles. On any normal day, she probably would've filled a cart with goodies to take home with her, but now, she walked around the miniature Eiffel Towers and maps and French flags and Versailles snow globes, taking it all in with little interest. What she was looking for, instead, was a way in.

She focused in on another entrance, past the registers, coming from the palace itself. People finishing with their tours were emptied out into the gift shop before leaving, so that they could make their purchases before heading to their tour buses.

Casually, she made her way over to it, pretending to look at a rack of postcards while watching the clerks at the checkout desk. There were two there, handling a long line of customers.

She took a deep breath, waiting. The second one of them turned to grab a bag and the other faced away from the door to give another visitor directions, Diana quickly squeezed out the door, disappearing into the crowd.

When she got far enough away from the gift shop, she looked back. No security guards were coming after her. She'd done it.

She let out the breath she'd been holding and walked in the opposite direction of the tour groups, skirting along the edge of the exhibits so as to call as little attention as possible to herself. She remembered the restrooms across from Chevrolet's office, so she walked that way, pausing in front of it. Streams of people were coming in and out of the door, so she simply side-stepped her way across the hall, pushing open the door that said, *pas d' admission sans affair.*

Inside, the vast office was dark. Diana closed the door behind her, scanning the room, letting her eyes adjust to the lack of light. When she could see reasonably well, she crossed to the desk and looked over the desk.

He'd cleaned it recently. Now, the papers and reports of incidents at the ball were gone. She spun around and faced a filing cabinet she hadn't really taken much notice of before. Holding her breath, she pulled on the handle, and it slipped open to reveal hundreds and hundreds of manila folders, all neatly organized.

Just looking at them all made her dizzy, not that she could see what they were in the minimal light. She strained to read the first one, then gave up, went to the desk, and pulled the chain on the lamp, casting the room into warm light.

Quickly, she started to rifle through the papers. But everything was in French or had a name on it, and none of it meant anything to her. *I will seriously be here forever if I have to go through all this.*

Wondering whether there was an easier way, she'd just begun to close the cabinet when she heard an audible click coming from the doorway.

She looked up to see Blaise Chevrolet staring at her, hand on the doorknob, a questioning look on his face. *"Qu'est-ce que tu fais ici?"*

*

She could've lied. There were about a dozen of them, bubbling at the tip of her tongue, but every one of them seemed inadequate. After

148

all of her strange behavior, he'd likely had his suspicions, but now, she'd been caught with her hand in the cookie jar. Nothing would get her out of this.

"Hello," she said, slamming the file folder closed.

"Madame St. James," he said, closing the door and crossing his arms. "I hope you realize that what you're doing—in my private office—is illegal. I could call the police and have you arrested."

"I understand. I wanted to come to you, but they said you weren't in," she said, hoping to throw a little bit of a guilt trip on him.

"*Oui*, well, I've been busy. I thought yesterday there was something in my office you were interested. But what I don't understand is . . . why?"

"You don't understand why?" She nearly laughed at that. "Really? In case you didn't notice, the police think I stole that necklace, and I'm on the hook for it. Not to mention that they think I murdered some man I don't even know. So pardon me if I'm interested in getting answers."

"What kind of answers do you think you'll find in my office?"

"I think I know who stole the necklace."

His eyes widened for a moment, but quickly, the doubt seeped in. "And how do you know that?"

"Because I was wearing it, remember? And I remember seeing a man, a man with a very distinct mask. It was black . . . with gold accents . . . and surprised eyebrows?"

"How do you know—"

"Because he helped me when I fell on the balcony stairs. I was wearing the necklace right before that, and it was gone—right after. I'm sure it's him." She motioned to his files. "So do you have information about who rented what pieces? Can you tell based on that?"

He nodded, "I can. It might take a while. We rented out over a thousand masks that night. Let me see."

She let out a sigh of relief as he went to the cabinet and pulled out a thick file of paper. He started to go through the pages. "Usually, we'd have this in our computer, but our computers were down the whole week, so we had to resort to paper." He started sorting through the pages. "Each form is a mask rental. This is private information. I could lose my job if anyone knew I was sharing this with you."

"I promise, I—"

He waved her off. "Let me just get it, and then you and I can pretend we never talked."

Diana didn't dare say anything. He was actually helping her, and she was afraid one wrong move could change his mind and make him call the police. She let him go through the pages, watching over his shoulder, until he pulled a paper out. "Black mask with gold scrolling, male. Here it is. Is this what you saw?"

She stared at it. There was a photograph of the item clipped to the paper. "Yes! That's it. Who does it belong to?"

He studied it. She moved closer, trying to read the name and address. *Leo Linville, 47 rue La Boétie *3, 8.* "You really think that this person stole the necklace from you?"

She nodded. "I'm almost positive."

"All right," he mused. "Well, I'll call the police and get them—"

Suddenly, he stopped and snapped the file shut, glaring at her over his bifocals.

"Mme St. James. What are you thinking you can do? This is a matter for the police, and only the police."

She shrugged innocently. "I would never do any—"

"Right. Just like you would never break into anyone's private office," he said, sitting back in his chair and dragging a hand down his face. "Please, Mme St. James, let me handle this. You do not need to be getting involved."

She frowned. The police's way of handling it would be going to the guy's house, asking him a few questions, and then letting him go free. They'd never find the necklace by playing by the rules and trusting the man's word on things.

No. Desperate times called for desperate measures.

And Diana had already flirted with breaking the law a few times, and she'd come out just fine.

Once more wouldn't make that much of a difference.

CHAPTER TWENTY SIX

Diana got it in her head that Leo Linville, the possible culprit, lived at *rue La Bowtie,* so, of course, the man in the shuttle looked at her like she had three heads.

Then it was like a light bulb went off in his head, and he said, "Do you mean *La Boétie?"*

She nodded. "Yeah. I think."

"Well, I have to get back to the hotel, but it's close by . . ."

"Great. You don't have to drop me off right in front. If you could just drop me anywhere around there, that would be fine," she assured him, rubbing her hands together. Her heart was beating like crazy as she thought of her next steps.

True to his word, the driver dropped her at a street corner, in a busy intersection. She quickly jumped out and headed down the street, trying to find the number for his house. At forty-seven, she stopped and looked inside the glass door. It was an apartment building.

She pulled on the door, expecting it to be closed, but it opened with ease. She went inside and found herself in a lobby with a few mailboxes. They were named. The third one said: *L. Linville.* There was also an intercom button next to it.

She almost pressed it. She had her finger, hovering over the button, ready to go. But what would she say to him? *Hello, WHERE IS THE NECKLACE?*

That wouldn't work. She'd have to be more subtle than that.

There was another glass door, and beyond that, a narrow hallway that stretched down the middle of the building, with two doors on each side. From the door, she spied Leo Linville's apartment at the very end on the left. She tried the interior door, but that was locked.

Diana went back out onto the street. Maybe she should give up and let the police handle it. After all, they were the experienced ones.

But she was the one here, now. And when she noticed a very narrow alley to the left of the building, she decided to take a trip down there and see where it led.

The aisle was so narrow, she almost had to move sideways in order to make it comfortably through. She had to climb over a few garbage cans, heavy with the stench of spoiled and rotten food. But as she'd expected, there were windows on this side. She passed several of them for the first apartment on that side, all closed.

When she reached another set, though, she found herself staring in on someone's kitchen. At a man, standing at the counter, slathering butter on a roll with a kitchen knife.

He started to turn, and she gasped and ducked down—just in time. She watched him, at the sink, cleaning his knife, and thought back to that instance on the balcony stairs. The man had been rather thick, but not fat. Built, solid and stout. He'd had a layer of brown stubble on his jaw and oddly fat lips like two sausages . . . Botox gone wrong.

Yes. This was Leo Linville. The man who helped her that night.

The man who'd stolen her necklace.

She looked around. Her situation had really not improved. What was she hoping to do? Break into his kitchen window and say, *Aha! I got you! I caught you red-handed.*

She hadn't caught anything. He didn't have the jewels on his person, as far as she could see. Didn't exactly strike her as the type to wear them around. Maybe, he'd even sold them already.

No, what you need, Diana, is good, solid proof. Then you can go on accusing him all you like.

But that was easier said than done. She stepped away from the house, scanning up it. There was an old trellis, swallowed mostly by ivy, and beyond that . . . another window.

An *open* window.

Aha.

She stood there, gauging the climb. She'd climbed the rope in high school gym class—only about thirty years ago. This would be like that. Sure.

Then, wiping her sweaty palms on the thighs of her pants, she looked up and down the alley to make sure no one was watching her.

All clear.

Are you going to do this, Diana? Or are you going to leave your fate in the hands of Inspector Clouseau?

Fastening the strap of her purse over her head, she rushed the trellis like a bear attacking its prey, digging her hands into the ivy, grabbing hold, and pulling herself up. She was surprised she still had it, whatever it was. When she got about three feet off the ground, she told herself, *Hey, this isn't so bad.* But then she looked up, and the window seemed farther away than ever. Was it moving?

This is really *not how I expected my first week in Europe to go.*

Sweat beading on her brow, she lifted her foot and dug it higher, seeking out the next rung among the foliage. A bee buzzed in her ear. Splinters stuck in her fingers. A wind blew her hair in her face, and she was glad she wasn't wearing a skirt. She went higher and higher, and it was right when she could nearly reach the bottom of the windowsill that she fully recognized it: *I have lost my mind. I am dangling on the edge of a building—about to break into a stranger's house.*

Somehow, that realization didn't stop her. With a last burst of energy, she grabbed ahold of the windowsill and hoisted herself up.

She was panting when she threw herself inside, but she tried to keep her heavy breathing to a minimum. Of course, the second she tried to straighten up and look around the room, the floorboards creaked. She winced.

It was a bedroom, and that was a good thing because she'd already decided that if the necklace would be anywhere, it'd probably be here. But if Leo was smart, he'd likely hide it—and hide it well, just in case anyone came looking.

She went to a dresser and pulled open the top drawer. Socks. The next drawer. Underwear.

Just when she thought this search would be absolutely fruitless, when she decided that there were far too many places that necklace could be, she peered in a little wooden box atop the dresser and found it. It looked almost costume, among a number of different baubles, but she knew it well because she and it had been very intimately acquainted that night.

The necklace. It was there, big and beautiful and shining in the sunlight streaming through the window.

She let out a little gasp of excitement. She couldn't believe her luck.

But then she looked closer. She lifted it up, and frowned. No. She'd worn the Madame Royale. This was nothing of the kind, light as air. Aside from the ruby-colored stone, it didn't even look similar. In fact, it wasn't even a necklace, just a piece of painted gold costume jewelry.

Before she could toss it back, the floorboards creaked behind her. She whirled slowly to find Leo Linville, standing in the doorway, staring at her.

Holding the kitchen knife in his fist.

For the third time since she'd arrived in France, she heard the magic words: *"Qu'est-ce que tu fais ici?"* *What are you doing here?*

She had to wonder that herself.

Because now, she was in some *really* deep trouble.

CHAPTER TWENTY SEVEN

What does one say when they're found snooping in a stranger's bedroom?

"Uh . . . hello," Diana said, backing toward the window, her eyes trained on the knife. "I think you have something that doesn't belong to you."

The man's sausage lips split into a yellow smile as he looked at her hand, still caught in his drawer. "I don't know what you're talking about, American. What are you trying to do?"

"Give me the necklace, and I won't cause any trouble."

"Seems to me like you're *already* causing trouble." He glanced toward the window. "You climbed all the way up to my bedroom—broke in?"

"W-well, the window was open, so technically, I just *slipped* in," she babbled, willing her brain to think of what to do next. *Diana, stop with the technicalities.*

"You *did* slip. This was probably the biggest slip you've ever made. Because you know I can't let you leave here."

She reached into her purse and pulled out her phone. "Put the knife away. I'll—I'll call the police."

"You try," he said, his voice low and menacing, "And just see what happens."

Okay, that was a threat. And she probably didn't really need any more of those, considering that knife he had seemed to be growing bigger and scarier the longer she stood there. It glinted in the sunlight coming through the window, taunting her. "Just give me the necklace. I'll leave, and it'll all be over. Okay?"

"*You* broke in here," he said. "The police will be on my side. Besides, I don't even know what necklace you're talking about."

How could he not? "The Madame Royale. I know it's here, somewhere."

He scoffed, "You're barking up the wrong tree, woman."

"You have to have it. The police know I didn't have it—they searched me. But *you* . . ."

His face twisted, and for a split second, the second that he tightened his grip on the knife and lunged over the bed for her, she regretted egging him on. She cringed and backed around the bed, toward the window, holding her hands up in defense.

But suddenly, a man in a gray blazer jumped onto the windowsill and pounced, putting his body between Diana and the thief. He started shouting, "*Arrestez!*" and a number of other commands Diana couldn't make out, holding his gun at the ready.

Diana's body sagged in relief. She let out a gasp of exhilaration, "Clouseau!"

He looked back at her for a moment, confused, then ripped his handcuffs from his belt. As he expertly whirled Leo around and cuffed him, he looked over at her, "What did you call me?"

"Oh. Nothing, lieutenant," she said, looking around for some way to change the subject. "I know this man stole the necklace. It's here somewhere. I'm sure of it."

Bayans looked around. "And what are you doing here?"

"Well, I—" She stammered. "Funny story. The man who helped me on the balcony was wearing a distinctive mask. Chevrolet gave me his information. Leo Linville. It has to be him. He was the only one who had the opportunity to steal the necklace. I'm sure of it." But now, as she gazed around his empty room, she *wasn't* so sure. And she was definitely trespassing. "How did you know to come here? Did Chevrolet tell you where I went?"

"No. We've been following you since it happened, Madame. We suspected from the beginning that you were a mark. A foreign woman, all alone in a strange country . . . it made you an easy target. We suspected someone was working with the murder victim to steal the necklace, and things went awry. We think someone killed the victim and made off with the necklace."

"Hey! That's nonsense! I'm no murderer!" the man shouted, his face contorted and red with rage.

"Well, why don't you and I go on downtown for questioning. Meanwhile, my men are going to search this place from top to bottom," he said, leading him out.

Diana followed him, head down. Well, of course she was just a mark. Of course the romance with Luc was just a silly ruse. She should've known. At her age, it was probably not best to believe that fairy tales and happily-ever-afters could come true.

They went outside to where his police car was waiting, and he shoved Leo Linville into the back. "Oh, Lieutenant," she asked him as he headed for the driver's side.

"Yes?"

"About that breaking and entering thing . . ."

He shrugged. "*What* breaking and entering thing? Just promise me you'll stay out of things from now on?"

She looked around, hoping the necklace would jump out at her. "Well . . . I'd really like to know if you find the Madame Royale. You'll tell me, right? It has to be here, somewhere. Or . . . maybe we're too late? Maybe he already sold it?"

Bayans rolled his eyes to the heavens. "I will be sure to let you know the moment we find it. But here, I thought you'd never want to hear about that confounded jewel again?"

She smiled. He was right. Jewelry was lovely, but that priceless artifact was a little too much for her. She'd be happy once this was all behind her.

But right now, it didn't feel like it was.

*

Diana thought she'd feel a lot better about things. Now, the blame was off her. Soon, they'd find the necklace. Likely, she'd no longer have to worry about rotting away in a French jail. Her retirement would remain intact. She still had weeks and weeks of adventure in Europe to enjoy. She should've been floating back to the inn on air.

And yet, as she walked down the streets of the city she'd always dreamed of seeing, something was wrong.

Stop it, she told herself. *Now, you can truly let the good times roll and enjoy this year abroad. Go to that café. Enjoy the food. See the Eiffel Tower and be HAPPY!*

She couldn't put her finger on just what it was, but something was bothering her. Maybe it was that after all her dreaming of the Versailles ball, she'd wound up in a fairy tale-turned-nightmare. Maybe it was that her Paris itinerary had been completely decimated.

But that wasn't it. Sure, "Luc" had been a dud, but it was nice even for those few moments to feel like she was in a fairy tale. And so what if she hadn't done everything on her itinerary? She was here, seeing it all. Just in a different, more frantic, less touristy way than she'd expected to . . . but she was having an adventure.

So . . . what was the problem?

She walked a few more blocks back to the hotel, peering in windows of shops selling fine French perfumes or delicate china and soap and housewares. As she did, the events of the past few days cycled through her head. So Claude and this man, Leo, had been in cahoots, working together to steal from the unsuspecting partygoers. Leo had snatched the necklace from her when she'd tripped on the balcony. Funny how she'd never even felt it! He must've been a pro . . .

Her phone pinged with a text. From Bayans. It said, *We've searched his place. No necklace yet.*

Perfect. She texted back, *What does that mean for me?*

Relax. He may have sold it off already. We're still working on it.

Relax? Not possible. She stopped, peering into a window at a little café. Her eyes went wide as a thought came to her.

Leo had come from *inside* the palace. She was sure of that fact—because the door had opened at her back, and he'd appeared behind her.

If that was true, then how could he have pushed Claude over the balcony railing and gone back into the palace only to reemerge again, all before the body was found?

Every hair on the back of her neck stood at attention as one thought came crashing down upon her, *He couldn't have.*

And that meant that someone else must have murdered Claude.

Maybe Leo was working on his own. Maybe Claude was working with someone else, and that person had gotten into a fight with him, possibly about not getting the necklace from her, and killed him. But who?

Everyone had looked at the necklace with interest. It had caught a lot of attention. Especially since she was the first person to be allowed to wear it at the ball. The sheer idea of giving something that expensive to just anyone to wear was actually kind of . . . crazy.

Insane.

Her mouth opened slightly. *I was only wearing that necklace because of . . .*

When the answer came to her, her breath caught in her throat. At that moment, she was looking at her reflection, not noticing that there was a man in the café window, about to eat a croissant, giving her an evil eye. She quickly averted her eyes and broke into a run.

She had to get back to Versailles.

CHAPTER TWENTY EIGHT

Diana grabbed the first cab she was able to hail, thanking the superb cab-stopping skills she'd acquired from living in New York. She climbed inside and shouted, "Versailles!"

The man in the driver's seat looked at her with suspicion, then sighed and began to pull away from the curb at a far too leisurely pace for Diana's liking.

"Step on it!" she barked, drumming her fingers on the armrest as she sat at the edge of the seat.

He gave her a dirty look in the rearview mirror. She cringed.

"I mean, please. I'm in a rush."

The shaggy-haired guy rolled his eyes and seemed to go *slower*. He even stopped at a red light most New York City drivers would've easily sailed right through. Yes, likely, dressed as a tourist in jeans and a t-shirt, she didn't have the look of someone who had pressing engagements. She gnawed on her lip, counting the moments for the light to change.

When it did, and he crawled ahead at a snail's pace, she leaned over and said, "Look. I think I know who murdered the guy at the Versailles ball. You know? The ball?"

The driver's eyes narrowed. *"Le meurtrier?"*

She nodded, "Yes! Yes, right. *Le meurtrier.*"

His jaw dropped, and he mimed, with great amusement, shoving someone. Then he pretended to flail and fall, waving his hands and screaming, "Ahhhhhh!" Then he looked at her, a question on his face.

"Yes. That's right. That's the one. I was at the ball. And I know who did it."

"Ah!" he said, and slammed so hard on the gas that Diana's body went flying against the vinyl seat back. He swerved, just missing a crossing pedestrian as he barreled a hard right around a corner.

The rest of the trip went by in a blur, with all the sights out the window fading together like the paints from a watercolor left out in the rain. Diana dug her fingernails into the armrest and held on for dear

160

life. The driver only stopped, and barely, when they reached the traffic outside the gate of the palace.

"This is good! I'll get out here!" Diana said and swiped her card.

The man, who clearly wanted to be in on the action, let out a groan, but she'd already pushed open the door.

"Thank you!" she called, slamming the door and rushing up the drive.

Despite having been here a number of times, she'd forgotten how long the roadway was between the gates and the entrance to the palace. She ran as fast as she ever had, weaving around tourists stepping off of their buses. By the time she got to the main fountain in front of the palace, she had nearly run a half a mile, and she had a stitch in her side.

She climbed the steps and went inside to the ticket desk. "Hello. I need to speak to Monsieur Chevrolet, the concierge, please," she said hurriedly.

The man behind the desk looked her over. "And who are you?"

Diana was about to answer when she noticed a man passing through the turnstiles at the other side of the vestibule. It was Chevrolet, and he was carrying a small satchel, kind of like a bowling bag. His eyes darted about for a moment like he was up to no good. *What is he up to?* she wondered, stepping away from the ticket desk and following him outside.

Once there, he started to pick up his pace. She tried to keep up—but was so out of breath from her jog that he quickly started to put distance between them.

Stopping, she shouted, breathless, "Monsieur Chevrolet!"

He stopped and turned, his eyes widening with surprise. She jogged up to meet him.

"Mon cher mademoiselle," he said, much less enthused than he ever had been before. "What brings you here again? I hope you're not trying to break into my office again?"

"No. Actually, I came to make sure you got the necklace back. And to see if you had any news about my wrap?" she asked.

"Yes. Everything's great. We got the necklace back where it belongs. No harm, no foul," he smiled in a way that seemed false. "Thank you for all your help."

Her eyes trailed to the bag. She couldn't help thinking that somehow, he was planning to run away with the necklace. What was he going to do? The inspector knew it was found. But there was definitely

161

something "off" about the way he was acting. Was he thinking he could just run off with it—in broad daylight?

"Yes, so . . . anyway," she said, reaching into her pocket for her phone. She fumbled with it, peeking at the display, trying to find the number for the police. "About my wrap. Did you find it?"

He looked away, at the exit, as if he couldn't wait to get here. He started to back away. "Uh, sorry. No. But like I said, if we do, we have your—"

"Thanks." She followed close to him, sticking to him like glue as he headed for the parking lot. "So where are you going? Lunch?"

He nodded. "*Oui.* Late lunch. I also have some errands to—"

"Oh. Can I come with you?" she asked with a shrug.

He stopped and looked at her. "Why?"

"Well, just to get a taste of Paris. From a local's perspective? I like to do that from time

to—"

"No," he said, cutting her off and stopping at the edge of the parking lot. "I'm sorry. I'm far too busy."

He began to walk again, this time at a faster pace.

Diana hesitated there, just long enough to grab her phone and punch in the call to Lieutenant Bayans. When he answered, she whispered, "Lieutenant. This is Diana St. James. I'm at Versailles with the real murderer."

"What?"

"You heard me! At Versailles!" She ended the call.

By then, Chevrolet had raced ahead. She tore after him, into a remote lot that must've been reserved only for staff. When he reached his car and began unlocking it, he glanced at her, scowling, "What are you—"

She rushed up to meet him, smiling. "Sorry. Hi again. So when do you think you will be back so I can come and look for my wrap?"

He placed the bag in the passenger seat of his car and straightened, clearly annoyed, "Like I said, I will call you if we find your—"

"I know you *said* that," she tittered, glancing toward the gates. She didn't see any sign of Bayans anywhere. "But I really feel like maybe whoever is working there isn't really looking. Or maybe doesn't know what to look for! And I think that if I just had a chance to—"

He shook his head. "I'm afraid that's impossible. And now you've wasted too much of my time. *Au revoir.*"

He started to sit down in his car and pull the door closed, but she clamped a hand on the frame, keeping it open. Desperately, she shouted, "Show me what you have in that bag!"

Chevrolet froze, "What?"

"You have that necklace in the bag. Admit it. You're going to . . . I don't know. Sell it to a fencer or something. You're stealing it."

His face reddened, the incredulous look only growing, "Are you insane?"

"If you have nothing to hide, you should be able to show me."

"I don't have time for thi—"

"You were in cahoots with Claude Lachance, weren't you? You arranged with him that you would put the necklace on some unsuspecting woman, and he would romance it right off of her. Right? But then what happened?"

She'd hoped he'd break down, admitting the crime. Instead, he did something she did not expect. He started to laugh—in a bitter way that made her spine tingle.

"You know nothing, American," he spat, glaring at her hand on his car door. "Go back to your hotel and leave me alone."

He tried to yank the door closed, but she held tighter. "I know it was you," she growled under her breath.

He laughed some more, then stood up, coming to his full height in front of her, the car door between them. His face was a scowl, his eyes narrowed to slits, "You do, do you?"

How had she never noticed he was this tall? This . . . intimidating? Parts of her were itching to run away, but the less sane part of her held tight to the door. She forced her chin up, meeting his stare, "Yes."

Suddenly, he reached out, grabbing her arm and wrenching it tightly. He pulled open the back door. "Get in."

She dug her feet into the pavement and tried to move backwards, but he had her tight in his grip. "Uh . . . what?"

"You heard me." He shoved her toward the open back door of the car. "You couldn't leave well enough alone, could you?"

"Where are you . . . what are you going to do?"

"You want to play detective? Let's play detective," he barked, prying her fingers off the door frame. "Let's you and I go for a little ride."

CHAPTER TWENTY NINE

This was definitely not on my itinerary, Diana thought as the crazy concierge tried to shove her into the back of his car. Diana stumbled forward, her knees hitting the seat, and sprawled out on the back seat.

Her heart raced. Working in the city, she'd heard that little safety tidbit a thousand times before: *Never let them take you to a second location. If you do that, you're as good as dead.* And that's what he was doing, much to her disbelief . . . kidnapping her.

Kidnapping me. Oh, my god. This wouldn't end well.

"Wait!" she shouted. Climbing to her knees, she started to scramble out. He tried to slam the door, but her feet were in the way. She struggled to keep it open, kicking her legs with all her might. There were people nearby, maybe not in the lot, but closer to the palace. If she could somehow alert them . . .

She screamed, as long and loud as she possibly could.

"Ferme ta gueule!" he growled, reaching forward to clamp a hand over her mouth. She lifted her arm to block it, elbowing him out of the way, and screamed again.

"Shut up!"

Shoving the door with all her might, Diana managed to kick him, hard, in the groin. He staggered backwards, clutching at his center and moaning, his face red and spittle flying from his mouth.

Hardly able to believe she was nearly free, she started to climb out, but then she remembered the bag, lying in the passenger seat. She reached between the front seats and grabbed ahold of it. She'd just begun to slip out when he wrapped his hands around her ankles and started to try to slam the door on her, effectively closing her in. One hard shove, and she heard the door click closed behind her.

This is it. It's over. I am done for.

Suddenly, a siren blared.

She looked over and let out a sigh of relief. Lieutenant Bayans was approaching in his squad car, with another one following. He pulled up directly behind Chevrolet's car, effectively prohibiting his vehicle from moving.

Chevrolet mumbled a curse and punched the air. He murmured something to Diana that probably wasn't anything nice and raked both hands through his hair. As he did, Bayans came around the squad car, hand on his firearm at his hip. "Now, what do we have here?"

Diana opened the bowling bag and reached inside. "He was going to steal this!"

But as she pawed around inside it, her stomach dropped lower and lower. The necklace wasn't there. Instead, she pulled out his passport, a few items of clothing . . . and the Rolex.

Well, at least there was that.

Bayans took the watch in his hand. "Planning on going somewhere with this?"

Chevrolet merely scowled.

"So *you* were the one working with Claude Lachance?" Bayans asked. "What about Linville?"

Chevrolet shrugged. "*Everyone* wants the Madame Royale. He was a competitor of ours. It was Lachance's idea—I put the necklace on some naïve tourist, and Claude was supposed to charm her and make off with it. Only he didn't have it when we met. I accused him of holding out on me, went through his pockets looking for it, and found the watch. Then we got into a little shoving match, and I must've pushed too hard." He shrugged. "What can I say? I never trusted the man. He was *un idiot*, anyway."

"But the necklace?" Diana demanded. "Where is the necklace?"

He shrugged. "Like I said. He didn't have it."

Diana frowned. "That has to be a lie. Where is it?"

Chevrolet smiled at her frustration. "You are a very good actress. Detectives, if I were you, I'd be looking at the American. She is more cunning than all of us."

Diana's jaw dropped. After all this, to have suspicion swing back to her? She couldn't take it. "What?"

Bayans motioned to the officers to take care of him, and as they came forward, bending him over the hood of his car and cuffing him, Chevrolet glared at Diana.

Un idiot, Diana thought. *Like me. I was the one who fell for his tricks, hook, line, and sinker. At least he wasn't an axe-murderer, or I might have never lived to tell this tale.*

She leaned against the car, hugging herself, and let out a sigh as the police dragged Chevrolet away. If the necklace wasn't with Chevrolet or Linville, she was out of ideas. She rubbed the goosebumps from her arms, feeling just as confused and shell-shocked as she did on that day that she'd witnessed the murder. She'd felt so cold, until that woman had brought that tea to warm her up, and . . .

Could it possibly be?

Bayans came over to her.

"Marie Antoinette!" she cried.

"Who?"

"The woman! On the balcony! Dressed like Marie Antoinette!"

He chuckled, "Mme St. James, there were about thirty women dressed like—"

"Yes. But the old lady! Remember? She'd put her arm around me, and . . . it has to be her!"

Bayans stared. Yes, she probably should've looked before she leapt, considering her last two ideas for the necklace hadn't really panned out, but this time, everything seemed to fall into place. And it seemed to be doing so for Bayans, too. He eagerly paged through his notepad. "Charlotte Bisset. Six *Rue de Cygnes, Paris.*" He snapped his fingers for the police, "Come on boys. We've got somewhere to be."

"Can I come?" she asked.

"Nice try," he headed for his patrol car. "Can I have an officer give you a ride back to your hotel, Mme St. James?"

As the patrol car drove off with Chevrolet inside, and she looked around, it hit her. She was free. And in the city of her dreams. And right now, there was absolutely nothing holding her back. No police or job obligations or romantic entanglements or weighty itinerary telling her where she needed to be at every moment. The sun was shining, and there was plenty of time left in the day. Everything she'd ever wanted was waiting for her, and all she had to do was seize it.

She smiled. "No. But I'll take a ride to Notre Dame, instead."

CHAPTER THIRTY

On her last day at *Le Bonne Auberge*, the newspapers blared the headlines: *Police a arrêté le voleur Madame Royale.* Yes, the police had found the woman, Charlotte Bisset, to be in possession of the necklace. In fact, she was wearing it when she answered the door for the police and was a bit confused. According to Bayans, the eighty-three-year-old woman may have been suffering from a bit of dementia, because she didn't seem to understand what had been going on. Her explanation? She couldn't remember how she'd gotten it and had just assumed it was a party favor.

Diana didn't care to argue. She was simply glad to put it all behind her.

Bright and early that morning, Diana signed her divorce papers, sealed the envelope, and left it with the concierge to send back to America. When she walked away from the papers, she felt strangely light. She wheeled her suitcase out to the curb and stood in the bright sunlight, feeling like she was at a crossroads. Another *Sliding Doors* moment—like whatever she did at this moment would have a profound effect on her.

As she stood there on the curb, taking in the beautiful blue sky and clouds dancing over the Seine and the stone bridges in the distance, someone tapped her on the shoulder. She whirled to see Sean standing beside her, newspaper in hand. He tipped his tweed flat cap at her. "So you are off, eh?" he asked, his eyes twinkling.

"Yes. I guess I am. Are you?"

"Nope. Not going back to old Ballygangargin quite yet. Thinking I'll tool around Europe, just like you. Let the wind take me where it takes me. How did Paris treat you, lass?"

Well, she could've probably spoken volumes on that. France hadn't been anything like she'd dreamed or expected. And yet, it had been an adventure. Something she would always remember, with a bit of fondness. No, she hadn't done a lot of what was on her itinerary, but that was fine. In fact, it was *perfect*. She wouldn't have done it any other way. And now, she couldn't wait for more. "It was great. I loved it."

He chuckled. "Yet another person who has fallen in love with this city. It gets its claws in you, I believe," he said. "So where does that itinerary say you're off to next?"

She was holding the bound book against her chest, but hadn't yet opened it. She wasn't really sure she wanted to. "I'm not going by that, anymore. I'm trying to decide."

"Ah. What are your choices?"

"I was thinking either Barcelona or Florence. What do you think?"

He shrugged. "Seems to me you can't go wrong with either. When I've got a choice like that, I flip a coin."

She laughed. Like she would ever leave such a monumental choice like that up to fate. "Thanks for the tip," she said, as the shuttle pulled up. "I hope I will see you again?"

He nodded, his eyes glinting with something like mischief. "I hope so, too. Let's count on it, why don't we? Until we meet again." He tipped his hat again and started to stroll off, then seemed to think better of it, because he reached into his pocket, pulled something out, and pressed it into her palm.

When she opened her hand, she found a coin there, unlike anything she'd ever seen before. It was old, and more octagonal than circular, with what looked like Gaelic runes upon it. Before she could ask him what it was, she looked up and realized he had gone.

The driver loaded her bags into the van, and she climbed inside, laying the itinerary on her lap. "Train station, please," she said to the driver.

As they moved through the mid-day traffic, Diana dared to open the cover and look at all the crossed-out, missed plans. All the forgotten dreams that had once been so important to her. That meal at that bistro, that in-depth tour she'd hoped to get at the Louvre. Funny, now that she looked at them, they hardly seemed to matter much at all.

She opened her palm and looked at the coin. *Heads, Florence. Tails, Barcelona.*

Was she really going to do this? Leave her journey up to fate, be like a feather in the wind?

Yes. She was surprised at how thrilling, how exciting the prospect was.

She tossed the coin. It landed heads. Her heart leapt as if it had known that was the right decision all along.

Florence, it is.

Diana stepped out onto the curb at the Metro station, grabbed her bags, and purchased a one-way ticket to Florence. She boarded the train, placed her bags in the overhead compartment, got herself situated in a window seat, and sat with her itinerary, looking at all the spoiled plans. Years ago, such a sight would've given her hives.

But now, she just smiled.

No, she hadn't seen the inside of the Louvre. But in her heart, she felt like she'd done something far better.

Then she flipped to the plans she'd made for Florence. A rigid schedule full of the same old things—things well-documented on any website or corner-store postcard, things that *anyone* could see.

She didn't want that anymore.

She crossed a big X through it and started over, on a clean page. Tapping her chin, she thought about the first thing she'd want to do, if she could do anything at all, in the beautiful city of Florence.

Her stomach rumbled, and she jotted, "Eat an authentic Italian meal."

Then she frowned. That would be nice, but if she was being honest with herself, it wasn't what was written on her heart. No, it wasn't even close. If she really wanted to write down things she desired for this trip, things that *mattered*, then a meal wasn't it. Not when there were so many other things out there to experience, things that weren't written on any map or guidebook.

She crossed it out and replaced it with, "Fall in love in Italy."

Yes. Much better.

And now, she was truly ready to go out and explore Europe, for all that it was worth.

NOW AVAILABLE!

DEATH IN FLORENCE
(A Year in Europe—Book 2)

"When you think that life cannot get better, Blake Pierce comes up with another masterpiece of thriller and mystery! This book is full of twists, and the end brings a surprising revelation. Strongly recommended for the permanent library of any reader who enjoys a very well-written thriller."
--Books and Movie Reviews (re *Almost Gone*)

DEATH IN FLORENCE is book #2 in a charming new cozy mystery series by USA Today bestselling author Blake Pierce, whose #1 bestseller *Once Gone* has received 1,500 five-star reviews. The series (A YEAR IN EUROPE) begins with book #1 (A MURDER IN PARIS).

Diana Hope, 55, is still adjusting to her recent separation when she discovers her ex-husband has just proposed to a woman 30 years younger. Secretly hoping they would reunite, Diana is devastated. She realizes the time has come to reimagine life without him—in fact, to reimagine her life, period.

Devoting the last 30 years of her life to being a dutiful wife and mother and to climbing the corporate ladder, Diana has been relentlessly driven, and has not taken a moment to do anything for herself. Now, the time has come.

Diana never forgot her first boyfriend, who begged her to join him for a year in Europe after college. She had wanted to go so badly, but it had seemed like a wild, romantic idea, and a gap year, she'd thought, would hinder her resume and career. But now, with her daughters grown, her husband gone, and her career no longer fulfilling, Diana realizes it's time for herself—and to take that romantic year in Europe she'd always dreamed of.

Diana prepares to embark on the year of her life, finally turning to her bucket list, hoping to tour the most beautiful sights and sample the most scrumptious cuisines—and maybe, even, to fall in love again. But a year in Europe may have different plans in store for her. Can A-type Diana learn to go with the flow, to be spontaneous, to let down her guard and to learn to truly enjoy life again?

In DEATH IN FLORENCE (Book #2), Diana arrives in Florence, ready to shake off the events of Paris and fulfill her lifelong dream of being proposed to on the romantic Ponte Vecchio bridge. But Diana can never possibly anticipate what she is about to find on that bridge, and how it may just turn her romantic dream into a ridiculous nightmare!

A YEAR IN EUROPE is a charming and laugh-out-loud cozy mystery series, packed with food and travel, with mysteries that will leave you on the edge of your seat, and with experiences that will leave you with a sense of wonder. As Diana embarks on her quixotic quest for love and meaning, you will find yourself falling in love and rooting for her. You will be in shock at the twists and turns her journey takes as she somehow finds herself at the center of a mystery, and must play amateur sleuth to solve it. Fans of books like *Eat, Pray, Love* and *Under the Tuscan Sun* have finally found the cozy mystery series they've been hoping for!

Book #3 (VENGEANCE IN VIENNA) in the series is now also available!

Blake Pierce

Blake Pierce is the USA Today bestselling author of the RILEY PAGE mystery series, which includes seventeen books. Blake Pierce is also the author of the MACKENZIE WHITE mystery series, comprising fourteen books; of the AVERY BLACK mystery series, comprising six books; of the KERI LOCKE mystery series, comprising five books; of the MAKING OF RILEY PAIGE mystery series, comprising six books; of the KATE WISE mystery series, comprising seven books; of the CHLOE FINE psychological suspense mystery, comprising six books; of the JESSE HUNT psychological suspense thriller series, comprising fifteen books (and counting); of the AU PAIR psychological suspense thriller series, comprising three books; of the ZOE PRIME mystery series, comprising six books; of the ADELE SHARP mystery series, comprising ten books (and counting); of the EUROPEAN VOYAGE cozy mystery series, comprising six books (and counting); of the new LAURA FROST FBI suspense thriller, comprising three books (and counting); of the new ELLA DARK FBI suspense thriller, comprising six books (and counting); of the A YEAR IN EUROPE cozy mystery series, comprising three books (and counting); of the AVA GOLD mystery series, comprising three books (and counting); and of the RACHEL GIFT mystery series, comprising three books (and counting).

An avid reader and lifelong fan of the mystery and thriller genres, Blake loves to hear from you, so please feel free to visit www.blakepierceauthor.com to learn more and stay in touch.

BOOKS BY BLAKE PIERCE

RACHEL GIFT MYSTERY SERIES
HER LAST WISH (Book #1)
HER LAST CHANCE (Book #2)
HER LAST HOPE (Book #3)

AVA GOLD MYSTERY SERIES
CITY OF PREY (Book #1)
CITY OF FEAR (Book #2)
CITY OF BONES (Book #3)

A YEAR IN EUROPE
A MURDER IN PARIS (Book #1)
DEATH IN FLORENCE (Book #2)
VENGEANCE IN VIENNA (Book #3)

ELLA DARK FBI SUSPENSE THRILLER
GIRL, ALONE (Book #1)
GIRL, TAKEN (Book #2)
GIRL, HUNTED (Book #3)
GIRL, SILENCED (Book #4)
GIRL, VANISHED (Book 5)
GIRL ERASED (Book #6)

LAURA FROST FBI SUSPENSE THRILLER
ALREADY GONE (Book #1)
ALREADY SEEN (Book #2)
ALREADY TRAPPED (Book #3)

EUROPEAN VOYAGE COZY MYSTERY SERIES
MURDER (AND BAKLAVA) (Book #1)
DEATH (AND APPLE STRUDEL) (Book #2)
CRIME (AND LAGER) (Book #3)
MISFORTUNE (AND GOUDA) (Book #4)
CALAMITY (AND A DANISH) (Book #5)
MAYHEM (AND HERRING) (Book #6)

ADELE SHARP MYSTERY SERIES
LEFT TO DIE (Book #1)

LEFT TO RUN (Book #2)
LEFT TO HIDE (Book #3)
LEFT TO KILL (Book #4)
LEFT TO MURDER (Book #5)
LEFT TO ENVY (Book #6)
LEFT TO LAPSE (Book #7)
LEFT TO VANISH (Book #8)
LEFT TO HUNT (Book #9)
LEFT TO FEAR (Book #10)

THE AU PAIR SERIES
ALMOST GONE (Book#1)
ALMOST LOST (Book #2)
ALMOST DEAD (Book #3)

ZOE PRIME MYSTERY SERIES
FACE OF DEATH (Book#1)
FACE OF MURDER (Book #2)
FACE OF FEAR (Book #3)
FACE OF MADNESS (Book #4)
FACE OF FURY (Book #5)
FACE OF DARKNESS (Book #6)

A JESSIE HUNT PSYCHOLOGICAL SUSPENSE SERIES
THE PERFECT WIFE (Book #1)
THE PERFECT BLOCK (Book #2)
THE PERFECT HOUSE (Book #3)
THE PERFECT SMILE (Book #4)
THE PERFECT LIE (Book #5)
THE PERFECT LOOK (Book #6)
THE PERFECT AFFAIR (Book #7)
THE PERFECT ALIBI (Book #8)
THE PERFECT NEIGHBOR (Book #9)
THE PERFECT DISGUISE (Book #10)
THE PERFECT SECRET (Book #11)
THE PERFECT FAÇADE (Book #12)
THE PERFECT IMPRESSION (Book #13)
THE PERFECT DECEIT (Book #14)
THE PERFECT MISTRESS (Book #15)

CHLOE FINE PSYCHOLOGICAL SUSPENSE SERIES
NEXT DOOR (Book #1)
A NEIGHBOR'S LIE (Book #2)
CUL DE SAC (Book #3)
SILENT NEIGHBOR (Book #4)
HOMECOMING (Book #5)
TINTED WINDOWS (Book #6)

KATE WISE MYSTERY SERIES
IF SHE KNEW (Book #1)
IF SHE SAW (Book #2)
IF SHE RAN (Book #3)
IF SHE HID (Book #4)
IF SHE FLED (Book #5)
IF SHE FEARED (Book #6)
IF SHE HEARD (Book #7)

THE MAKING OF RILEY PAIGE SERIES
WATCHING (Book #1)
WAITING (Book #2)
LURING (Book #3)
TAKING (Book #4)
STALKING (Book #5)
KILLING (Book #6)

RILEY PAIGE MYSTERY SERIES
ONCE GONE (Book #1)
ONCE TAKEN (Book #2)
ONCE CRAVED (Book #3)
ONCE LURED (Book #4)
ONCE HUNTED (Book #5)
ONCE PINED (Book #6)
ONCE FORSAKEN (Book #7)
ONCE COLD (Book #8)
ONCE STALKED (Book #9)
ONCE LOST (Book #10)
ONCE BURIED (Book #11)
ONCE BOUND (Book #12)

ONCE TRAPPED (Book #13)
ONCE DORMANT (Book #14)
ONCE SHUNNED (Book #15)
ONCE MISSED (Book #16)
ONCE CHOSEN (Book #17)

MACKENZIE WHITE MYSTERY SERIES
BEFORE HE KILLS (Book #1)
BEFORE HE SEES (Book #2)
BEFORE HE COVETS (Book #3)
BEFORE HE TAKES (Book #4)
BEFORE HE NEEDS (Book #5)
BEFORE HE FEELS (Book #6)
BEFORE HE SINS (Book #7)
BEFORE HE HUNTS (Book #8)
BEFORE HE PREYS (Book #9)
BEFORE HE LONGS (Book #10)
BEFORE HE LAPSES (Book #11)
BEFORE HE ENVIES (Book #12)
BEFORE HE STALKS (Book #13)
BEFORE HE HARMS (Book #14)

AVERY BLACK MYSTERY SERIES
CAUSE TO KILL (Book #1)
CAUSE TO RUN (Book #2)
CAUSE TO HIDE (Book #3)
CAUSE TO FEAR (Book #4)
CAUSE TO SAVE (Book #5)
CAUSE TO DREAD (Book #6)

KERI LOCKE MYSTERY SERIES
A TRACE OF DEATH (Book #1)
A TRACE OF MUDER (Book #2)
A TRACE OF VICE (Book #3)
A TRACE OF CRIME (Book #4)
A TRACE OF HOPE (Book #5)

Printed in Great Britain
by Amazon

41592938R00108